SINCE YOU LEFT ME

Other books by Allen Zadoff

Food, Girls, and Other Things I Can't Have

My Life, the Theater, and Other Tragedies

SINCE YOU LEFT ME

BY ALLEN ZADOFF

EGMONT
USA
New York

EGMONT

We bring stories to life

First published by Egmont USA, 2012
443 Park Avenue South, Suite 806
New York, NY 10016

Copyright © Allen Zadoff, 2012
All rights reserved

1 3 5 7 9 8 6 4 2

www.egmontusa.com
www.allenzadoff.com

Library of Congress Cataloging-in-Publication Data

Zadoff, Allen.
Since you left me : a novel / by Allen Zadoff.
p. cm.
Summary: "A Jewish teenager struggles to find something to believe in
and keep his family together in the cultural confusion of modern-day
Los Angeles"—Provided by publisher.
ISBN 978-1-60684-296-6 (hardback)—ISBN 978-1-60684-297-3 (e-book)
[1. Faith—Fiction. 2. Jews—United States—-Fiction. 3. Single-parent
families—Fiction. 4. High schools—Fiction. 5. Schools—Fiction.
6. Family life—California—Los Angeles—Fiction.
7. Los Angeles (Calif.)—Fiction.] I. Title.
PZ7.Z21Sin 2012
[Fic]—dc23
2012003782

Printed in the United States of America

Book design by ARLENE SCHLEIFER GOLDBERG

Acknowledgments

Special thanks to Danny Silberstein and Simon Lousky for sharing their experiences in and out of Jewish school (and teaching me about getting flipped).

Thanks to Taaly Silberstein for opening her home to me on many a Shabbat and for her beautiful example of what it means to live a Jewish life. Much thanks to Adam Silberstein for his incredible support, knowledge, and perspective.

Extra special thanks to Ira Gewanter for his early read of the manuscript.

As always, I'm very grateful to Stuart Krichevksy, Shana Cohen, and Ross Harris at SK for taking such good care of me.

Finally, a giant thanks to Elizabeth Law and the Egmont team for making book three together such a great experience.

An Israeli woman with large breasts is calling my name.

In most situations, an amply endowed woman with an accent who wants me for something—anything, really—is a good sign, but not tonight. Not in the high school gymnasium on the night we're having parent-professor conferences. And not when the woman shouting is the new office lady trying to tell me it's time for my conference.

That is not a good thing. Not at all.

"Sanskrit Aaron Zuckerman," she shouts.

That's my name, in all its confusing glory. She says the *Sanskrit* part like it's Hebrew, which is not a terrible guess given that we're at Brentwood Jewish Academy. B-Jew for short. That's what the students call it. The faculty does not appreciate the term.

But my name, Sanskrit, is not Hebrew. It's an ancient Indian language.

"Sanskroo . . . ," she says, garbling it.

When someone is looking in my direction and choking on a word, they're almost always trying to say my name. Or they have a piece of corned beef stuck in their throat. It's me or a choking incident.

"Zuckerman?" the woman calls out, opting for the familiar territory of my last name. "The professors are ready."

Professors. That's what we call them here, even though it's only high school. We're so college obsessed, we even use the nomenclature.

Now I can see the Israeli office lady pushing her way through the crowd. She's wearing her favorite outfit—a silky blouse that covers all of her skin yet leaves nothing to the imagination, and a long, too-tight skirt. Appropriate length. Inappropriate width. Which makes it all the more interesting.

If she's calling me, it's time for my mother to go in and meet the faculty.

Problem: my mother isn't here yet.

Solution: evasive action.

I duck behind Mrs. Rosenthal. That's easy to do because she is, shall we say, on the large side. When Moses climbed the mountain to get the tablets, I imagine the mountain looked something like Mrs. Rosenthal, only with a less attractive pantsuit. Mrs. Rosenthal is heading for a little nosh at the snacks table, and I move with her, using her ample girth as cover. I stay behind her until I get to Mrs. Stein, Talya's mom, and then I jump behind her until I get to Barry Goldwasser's parents. In this way, I hop-scotch across the gymnasium using large Jews as cover until I've put as much distance as possible between myself and my name.

I scan the room for my mother, hoping I've missed her.

I haven't.

I look at my phone. No calls, and she's over an hour late.

My mother promised she'd be here. It's just that she has a different definition of *promise* than the rest of the world. For her, it's a relative term.

Parent-professor conferences can be squirm-worthy in the best of circumstances, but they're especially problematic when your parents don't show up. Not that I'd expect both of my parents to be here at the same time. They haven't been in the same room in five years, unless you count my bar mitzvah. I've been try-ing to erase the memory of that day for years.

But Mom has to be here. That's because she missed the last one, along with just about every other school event, and we almost got expelled. I say "we" because they blame the whole family in our school. There's no such thing as a student alone—the student is an extension of the family. They call it the Critical Family Dynamic. I call it Guilt by Association.

In any case, we had to sign a Family Education Contract after that. It wasn't all Mom's fault. I blew off religious studies homework and skipped prayer four times in a month and got myself on academic probation. Basically, I was failing God.

Failing *HaShem*.

That's what we call God here. *HaShem. The Name* in Hebrew.

Anyway, I was already the dean's special remodeling project because of my lack of religious commitment, and Mom not showing up made it a thousand times worse. In the family contract, we each agreed to a list of responsibilities. On the top of Mom's list: stay engaged in the educational process by attending all meetings and conferences. On the top of mine: find God, or at least fake it well enough to get through Torah class and morning prayers.

I drift towards the edge of the gym, weaving my way through the families. Parents stand in clumps, some with their arms around their children. They're chatting and laughing, trying to look calm even though I can tell some of them are scared. Not every family got a good report about their child. You can feel the Ivy League hopes hanging in the balance. Not just Ivy. Yeshiva hopes, a year in Israel hopes. B-Jew hopes.

Parents and the dreams they have for their children.

I look at my watch. Where the hell is my mother?

The new office lady stalks through the crowd with

clipboard in hand, her angry breasts searching me out. She taps a kid on the shoulder.

"Where is Sanskrit?" she asks him.

The kid shrugs.

I move in the opposite direction, stalling for time.

I grab a knish and pretend I'm going to talk to someone I know. But I don't really have anyone to talk to. I'm not what you call a popular kid. I'm more of an outsider. All Jews are outsiders in a certain way, so you really have to work to be on the outside of the outsiders. Actually, it's not that difficult in Jewish school. All you have to do is not believe in God.

There are other kids who don't believe, but they do it quietly or couch it in intellectual inquiry. I do it openly and loudly. Add that to the fact I come from a family of divorce, I'm named after a dead *goyish* language, I have a yoga teacher for a mother and the Invisible Man for a father—you pretty much have the definition of outsider.

I look up and I see Herschel, my former best friend, in a full suit and black fedora moving amongst the parents. He's one of the few who dresses in religious garb in our school. Brentwood Jewish is an Orthodox school, but we're a lot more modern than most. Herschel isn't modern, not anymore. He's in it to win it. Today he works the room like a politician, smiling and shaking hands, patting various parents on the shoulders as if to calm them. He's comfortable with the parents, with the kids, with God. Especially with God. I wish I could believe like he does. Life would be so much simpler.

There's a tap on my shoulder.

"Sanskrit. Am I saying that right?"

The Israeli office lady. She found me.

I say, "It's *San* like *sand*. And *skrit* rhymes with *Brit*. Emphasis on the first syllable. *San*-skrit."

She looks at me like I'm an idiot, that special look Israelis have that makes you feel stupid because you're soft, and American, and haven't fired an UZI.

"Sanskrit," she says.

Heads turn. God, this woman is loud.

Most of these people know me, but even so, what's a Jew doing with a name like Sanskrit? It's the unspoken question everywhere I go.

The woman says, "We're ready for your parents."

"Parent. Singular," I say. "For your information, my mom is stuck in traffic. She'll be here shortly."

She wrinkles her nose.

"What about your father?"

"My parents are divorced."

The foundation of Jewish education is parent involvement.

That's what it says in our school brochure. It's also written on the wall outside the main office. It's on the letterhead of all the school newsletters.

Parent involvement.

"Even divorced parents come for conferences," the office lady says.

"If you look at my paperwork," I say.

She lifts the clipboard to chest level, and we both look at it. Actually, she's looking at the clipboard. I'm looking elsewhere.

She says, "Your father is listed as an alternate parent? *Mah zeh?* What is this?"

Alternate. That's code for, "Don't expect that parent to show up."

"My father is not expected to come to school events," I say.

"That's strange," she says.

"It's not so strange," I say.

"No? Maybe my English is not good with this word?"

I glance around the room. Half the parents are looking at me, and the other half are looking away. Which just means they're listening.

"Whatever," I say. "Could you let someone else go ahead of me?"

"You are the *Z*. There isn't anyone else."

I see Herschel's parents walking towards me.

"Give me two minutes," I tell the office lady, and I run towards the Weingartens.

Herschel's parents used to consider me a good influence on their son. We were close, we studied together, I got him out of the house. But now that he's their religious pride and joy, I am no longer considered a good influence. I am considered a dangerous, subversive influence. As such, I am no longer welcome around the Weingarten household with the exception of a few major holidays. It's not like they lock the doors and turn out the lights when they see me coming, but let's just say the Shabbat invitations are infrequent.

"Hello, Sanskrit," Mrs. Weingarten says. "Is everything all right?"

"Perfect," I say.

I glance behind me. The office lady has been temporarily swallowed up by the crowd.

"I wanted to say shalom to your mother."

"She hasn't arrived just yet," I say.

"I see," Mrs. Weingarten says. "I hope there's no problem."

"Maybe she left the country without telling me," I say.

"God forbid!" Mrs. Weingarten says.

"It was a joke," I say.

"Sanskrit is funny. Remember, Mom?" Herschel says.

He's swooped in from the side to spare me any more embarrassment. Very decent of him.

"Of course I remember," Mrs. Weingarten says. She nudges her husband. "You remember Sanskrit, don't you, Stanley?"

Stanley Weingarten nods his head. That's their entire relationship. Mrs. Weingarten talks and Mr.

Weingarten nods. Maybe that's the secret to staying married. If my father had nodded more, things would have worked out.

"Sanskrit, will we see you at Pesach this year?" Mrs. Weingarten says.

"Of course," I say. Usually, we'd be scarce on a big holiday like Passover, but the Family Education Contract means we need to make a show of it. I still haven't told Mom she's going to the Weingartens' seder next week. It's their once-yearly attempt to bring us back into the fold. I've learned you don't bring Mom bad news during a juice fast.

"We'll look forward to seeing you," Mrs. Weingarten says.

I reach for my pocket like my phone is vibrating.

"I think that's my mom now. Will you excuse me?" I say.

I walk away, checking my phone for the twenty-seventh time.

Not even a text.

I dial Mom again, and it goes directly to voice mail. Which means her phone still isn't on.

I start to feel angry. My mother knows how important this is. I've reminded her enough times.

Somehow she never misses a yoga class, either taking one or teaching one. But all other appointments are considered optional. Including mine. Which means I'm as forgettable as everyone else in Mom's life.

I check the time and see that Mom is now an hour and a half late.

Time for emergency action.

I call my little sister, Sweet Caroline. That's actually her name. Our parents had a deal that Mom got to name the first child, Dad the second. They each named us after their favorite things—Mom an ancient language and Dad an ancient Neil Diamond song.

Sanskrit and Sweet Caroline Zuckerman.

The seeds of divorce were planted early in our family.

"What do you want?" Sweet Caroline says when she answers the phone.

She doesn't even bother to say *hello*. That's how sweet she is.

"Where's Mom?" I say.

"How the hell should I know?"

"Watch your mouth."

"Right. Like you never swear."

"Caroline, please."

"Sweet," she says.

She hates it when I don't say her whole name. Unlike me, she's taken ownership of her name. She says it's cool to have a weird name in Los Angeles. It makes her feel like the daughter of famous actors.

"Caroline," I say again, because I'm angry, and maybe I want to take it out on her a little. That's what sisters are for.

"My name is *Sweet* Caroline," she says, "not *just* Caroline."

"It's not like you went to Sweet School and earned the title," I say.

"My father gave me this name and it's the name I will be called," she demands.

"Fine," I say.

"Fine," she says.

And she hangs up.

Jesus.

I dial her number again.

"What?" she says as if we didn't just talk.

"Hi, Sweet Caroline."

A pause.

"How can I help you?"

"Do you by any chance know where our mother is?" I say.

"Yoga center meeting," she says.

"How do you know?"

"Because I got home from gymnastics, and she texted me that there was curry tofu for dinner in the fridge. If she asks, we ate it and loved it."

"Could you look at her calendar?"

She moans.

"It's important," I say.

"What's so important?"

"Excuse me," a professor says as she walks through the gymnasium. "No cell phones."

B-Jew has a strict no-cell-phone policy. Strict is an understatement.

"I'm just calling my mother," I say to her. "It's an emergency."

"No. A bomb on a bus in Tel Aviv is an emergency. Your cell phone is a nuisance." She points to the door.

I run outside.

"Look at Mom's calendar, Sweet Caroline," I say. "Please. I'm in a bind here."

"What kind of bind?"

"A bad one."

"Details. I need details."

"Why?"

"Because I like to hear you suffering."

I think of a few choice things I'd like to say to her, but I keep them to myself.

"We've got parent-professor conferences tonight," I say.

"Ohhhh," Sweet Caroline says, like she understands without me saying another word.

I hear her walking into the kitchen. It sounds crazy, but I'm sort of hoping there's nothing on the calendar. Maybe Mom didn't forget. Maybe it's my fault because I forgot to remind her.

"The calendar says *juice fast*," Sweet Caroline says.

"That's it?"

"Wait. There's a big arrow pointing from today to a card on the refrigerator. *Parent-professor conference for Sanskrit. 5:30 p.m.* There are about fifteen exclamation marks."

"I know. I wrote it."

So Mom outright forgot. Or she remembered and didn't care enough to show up. Either way, I'm screwed.

"No Mom?" Sweet Caroline says.

"No Mom," I say.

"Did you call Dad?"

"Are you crazy?"

"He might come."

"Yeah, if I was in the emergency room."

"You're right. You are screwed," she says.

You'd expect a tiny bit of understanding from your own sister. It's not like I'm the only one who's ever been screwed over by Mom in our family. On her last birthday, Mom surprised Sweet Caroline with a vegan cake that said *Happy Eleventh!*

Slight problem: Sweet Caroline was twelve.

Despite it all, Sweet Caroline walks around like she doesn't have a problem in the world, like she's got a loving family that shows up for her no matter what. But she's got the same family I have. The one that has her picking at herself so much she got sent to a psychologist.

"Sanskrit?" she says.

"What?"

"Better you than me."

She hangs up.

I look back towards school. Herschel is coming out the front door, his suit panels flapping in the wind.

"What's happening here?" he says.

"I'm taking a cigarette break."

"Very funny. Where's your mom?"

"Two guesses. Both involve tights and a gong."

"Did you call her?"

"Forty-seven times."

"Your father?"

"Jesus, Herschel."

"Language," he says.

"I'm sorry. Jesus H. Christ, Esquire."

He looks at me deadpan.

That would have made him laugh in the old days. You're not supposed to take the Lord's name in vain, so when we swore, we'd add an honorific. Like instead of saying, "Oh, God!" we'd say, "Oh, *Doctor* God!" Or "God, *Master of the Universe*, damn it!"

In the old days it was funny. Herschel used to hate Jewish school as much as I did. That was before he went to Israel and got flipped. That's what we call it when kids visit Israel and find God. One look at the Western Wall, and they think they're Maimonides.

These days Herschel's sense of humor has been overwhelmed by the study of Torah. Not a lot of laughs in Torah class.

"Call your father," Herschel says.

"No."

"This is serious. You're on thin ice with the administration."

"Maybe this is my ticket out."

"We're all out after next year. Think about college," Herschel says. "Think about Brandeis."

A cramp seizes my stomach. Brandeis. A Jewish university without much Judaism, all the way on the other side of the country. My ticket to freedom. But I need the grades to get there.

"Do you want me to call your dad for you?" Herschel says.

"I'm a big boy," I say.

Just then Barry Goldwasser pokes his head out the back door.

"Sanskrit!" he shouts. "They're looking for you."

Here's Barry to save the day again. I swear, the guy thinks he's Jewish Superman. What's worse is that he knows I can't stand him, but he doesn't care. He's one of those guys who likes you even when you don't like him. Such is the incredible generosity of spirit by which he lives. It's nauseating.

"Could you tell them I'll be there in a minute?" I say.

Barry says, "Your family is in turmoil. You have to confront it sooner or later."

I flip Barry the bird.

"Look where your finger is pointing," he says.

I look up.

"God can handle your family problems, Sanskrit. Not me."

"Screw you, Barry. And screw God."

He shakes his head like I'm a lost cause.

I take a big step towards the door like I'm ready to fight Barry for my family's honor. But he's already gone.

"Can you believe that?" I say to Herschel.

"Your dad," he says, completely unfazed by Barry or anything else.

I stare at Dad's number on my phone. I imagine me asking—and Dad turning me down with a lame excuse like he usually does. It's too much for me right now.

I turn off the phone.

"What are you going to do?" Herschel says.

"Take the hit. Like I always do."

I walk back into the gym through the crowd of parents and students. They've all had their conferences now, but it's tradition to stick around and socialize until everyone's parents have had their turn. That means they're all waiting for me.

I glance at the snacks table. It's looking pretty scarce over there. Once the snacks run out, there will be a riot.

The Israeli office lady sees me and gestures for me to hurry.

I glance to my left, and I see a girl. Not just any girl.

The Initials.

In God's case, we don't say his name as a sign of respect. In her case, it's because it's too painful.

The Initials is standing with her parents. She looks gorgeous. Her mom looks gorgeous.

I catch myself staring, and I look away. It's like looking into the sun. If you become distracted by the majesty, you'll burn out your retinas.

"Sanskri—" the office lady starts to say.

"Coming," I say.

"Your mother?"

I shake my head.

Can breasts look disappointed? Maybe I'm imagining it.

"Follow me," she says, and we walk in silence down the hall.

She stops in front of the large conference room. She opens the door and holds it for me.

I step into the room.

All my professors are sitting there. They look past me to the door, expecting an adult to walk in behind me.

But it's just me.

"Aaron," the dean says. He always calls me by my middle name. The Jewish-sounding one. Sometimes he even pronounces it in Hebrew, like *Ah-roan*.

"You're not wearing your *kippah*," he says.

"Sorry," I say.

Kippot are required to be on our heads at all times in school. Some kids wear them out of school as well, but I don't like to wear mine at all, so I usually stuff it in my pocket.

I pull it out. I've got a tiny one the same color as my hair so you barely notice it.

"Where's your mother?" the dean says.

I look across the table of professors, all of them staring back at me. Professor Hirschberg glares at me below a severe unibrow. The dean sighs.

"We've talked about this numerous times," he says. "The Family Contract . . . "

I think about all the times I've made excuses for Mom, all the embarrassment I've suffered.

I'm ready to take the hit again. I always take the hit.

I'm about to apologize on Mom's behalf, when I'm overcome with anger. No more hits. No more embarrassment.

I don't tell the teachers that my mother forgot or that she's stuck in another appointment.

Instead I say, "There's been a terrible accident."

The entire room gasps. Professor Schwartzburg, my English teacher, clutches his chest. He's been doing that a lot lately. In fact, there's a betting pool on the next professor to have a heart attack, and Schwartzburg is in the lead.

I say, "I don't have all the details yet. I'm waiting to get an update from the hospital."

I don't know why I'm saying any of this, but I'm not exactly in my right mind. When I think about it later, I realize I should not have used the word *terrible* to describe the accident. It's hard to recover from *terrible*. If you say *accident* and you want to backtrack later and claim it was a fender bender, you're okay. But it's very hard to get from *terrible* back to *minor*.

But I tell the professors Mom was in a terrible accident, and after the initial shock and several *oy veys*, Professor Feldshuh leaps up and takes matters into his own hands.

"I'll give you a ride to the hospital!" he says.

I say, "No thank you, sir. I have a ride."

All the professors are on their feet then, reaching for me, patting my shoulder, offering their support, and asking if there's anything they can do.

"I have to go," I say. "Right now."

"I'll pray for you," Professor Skurnick says.

She puts a hand on her chest and pats herself. I make a quick note to check her rank in the heart attack pool.

Then I rush out of the room.

The Israeli office lady jumps out of my way.

I run back through the gymnasium. There are startled reactions all around me. Maybe they think something awful happened in my conference, like I'm being suspended or expelled.

I can't worry about it right now.

I keep my head down and rush out the door, inadvertently slamming it behind me.

Professor Schwartzburg says you should never end a sentence with an exclamation point. He calls it overkill.

But in life, ending with an exclamation point feels good.

I just never knew it before.

I hate my mother.

This is not a very Jewish thought to be having. Some might say it's a sin. After all, the commandment tells us, *Honor your mother and your father.* As Herschel says, "They're called the Ten Commandments, not the Ten Suggestions."

Honor. Maybe that was easier to do three thousand years ago.

It's not easy now. Not with my family.

I'm sitting in the dark in our kitchen waiting for Mom to come home. I'm supposed to be honoring her, but I hate her. I make a list in my head: Top Reasons I Hate My Mother. When I get to number twenty, I stop. The list is supposed to make me feel better, but the more things I add, the angrier I get.

I say out loud, "I don't care if my mother never comes home. I don't care if she was in a car accident for real. I don't care if she's gone forever."

Who am I talking to?

Not *HaShem*. You're not supposed to say bad things about people to God.

You don't wish your enemies dead, much less your own mother. Jews are craftier than that when it comes to their prayers. Jews wish their enemies *well*. For example, in Yiddish you say, *gey gezunt*, which means something like "Go in good health." You might say that to a friend or family member you love. But you can use the same phrase for someone you hate. If you say *gey gezunt* to someone you hate, it's like telling them to go to hell.

Maybe *HaShem* will appreciate that I'm speaking directly rather than cloaking my real thoughts in euphemisms. Maybe I'll get some credit for honesty.

But probably not.

Probably he's going to be pissed, and he's brewing up a special tragedy for me.

That's if I believed in God in the first place. If God doesn't exist, what does it matter what you say? You could say anything, do anything. And the 613 Jewish mitzvahs, the rules that every devout Jew is supposed to follow and around which we organize our lives? They might be just a waste of time.

That thought makes me all the more depressed.

I don't know what's worse, a God who punishes you for doing the wrong thing, or a God who doesn't care at all.

I pace back and forth in the kitchen. The clock says

9:30 p.m. It's not unusual for Mom to be out so late and have her phone off. She teaches night classes some- times or has meetings at the Center. We come home to some form of vegetarian stew in the refrigerator or a twenty-dollar bill on a plate on the table, partially cov- ered by a napkin with a heart drawn on it. Mom's not totally irresponsible. More like totally self-involved.

But for her to outright miss my conference with all that's been going on at school?

That's unusual.

Sweet Caroline wants nothing to do with any of this. She's already in bed reading or doing homework, com- pletely unperturbed by the fact that my life is falling apart. This is one of those times you want to present a united front as siblings. We could form a familial picket line, demand Mom be home at certain times, demand that she attend our events. Force her to stop cooking the stews. We could make this our last stand.

But Sweet Caroline and I haven't stood together in a long time. I can't even remember the last time we did anything together, just the two of us.

My phone buzzes.

It's my eighteenth call since leaving school. None of them have been from Mom.

Six of the messages have been from Herschel's num- ber. Another four from the main line at school. The rest of them from numbers I don't know. I listened to one, and it was a worried Professor Schwartzburg calling from his cell phone. Teachers *never* call students from their own phones.

Which means my lie really had an impact.

The phone vibrates and call number eighteen goes to voice mail.

On one level it's nice to know people care. On another level, I'm not sure anybody cares. They're doing a mitzvah, a good deed. In the face of tragedy, Jews snap into action. Someone is injured in a car accident, someone is sick, someone dies—we're there with phone calls, kind words, and noodle kugel.

Jews love tragedy. It's in our DNA.

It's the day-to-day stuff that proves more challenging.

Just then I hear Mom's key in the front door.

She walks in humming one of the meditation pieces she listens to constantly. I don't know the name of it. It's less a song than a chant that endlessly repeats itself until you either surrender to it or go insane.

Mom comes into the kitchen without noticing me. In one arm she has the Trader Joe's tote bag with her yoga mat tied to its side, and in the other she has a big bag of fluff-and-fold from the dry cleaners. Mom lets the wash stack up until she gets overwhelmed, then she has no choice but to spend money to have someone else do it. At least it gets done.

Mom drops the laundry on the floor, hums her way over to the refrigerator, and grabs a miniature carton of organic apple juice. She tears open the plastic on the straw with her teeth and pops it into the box of juice—

"Mom."

"Oh!" she shouts, and jumps back.

The box falls and shoots a splatter of droplets onto the floor.

"You scared me, Sanskrit," she said.

She takes three deep breaths, centering herself like she always does. Then she grabs a wet rag to clean the spill. No paper towels in our house. They're bad for the environment.

"Why are you sitting in the dark?" Mom says. "It's not good for your eyes."

"I'm waiting for you."

Mom scrunches her eyebrows. "Waiting for me to what?"

"Close the refrigerator door," I say.

She swings the door shut. Then she shrugs.

"Look on the door," I say.

"What am I looking at? Do we need miso?"

I flip on the kitchen light. I walk over and put my finger on the reminder card. Then I point to the Family Education Contract, stuck to the door with a karma boomerang magnet.

"Oh my gosh, is it Wednesday?" Mom says.

I nod.

"Sweetie, did I miss it?"

"You missed it."

"I'm so sorry. I'm out of my mind with this juice fast. Honestly, I don't know who I am right now. I'm running from classes to the bathroom and back. I'd give anything for a nice solid number two."

"Maybe food would help."

"Tomorrow," she says, her face lighting up. "My eleven days is up. I can't wait to chew something!"

Mom reaches down to clean up the spill. She doesn't bend over like a normal person. She drops into a squat, her butt practically hitting the floor.

"How did the school thing go?" she says to me. She slurps hard from the juice pack.

"Not well," I say. "It's difficult to have a parent-professor conference without a parent."

"Did you take notes?"

"You don't get it, Mom. It didn't happen."

"Why couldn't you do it and give me a report like you always do? Fill me in, honey. You're good at that."

"They don't tell me how I'm doing. They need a responsible adult for that."

"Why didn't you call me?" She takes out her phone and looks at it. "Oops. My phone was off. I didn't even realize it."

She turns it on.

"Mom, this is really serious. They're going to throw us out of school."

"Why would they do that? With the amount of money we pay?"

"You don't pay anything."

"You know what I mean," Mom says.

There's no way Mom could afford my school. Tuition this year was nearly thirty thousand dollars. Without Zadie Zuckerman's money, I'd be a public school kid, and Mom would be panicked about paying for college in two years. Mom hated Zadie Zuckerman and she refuses to admit his money is still running our life. It's not just my education money either. If Zadie hadn't bought this house when my parents got married, we'd be living in an apartment in some crappy suburb instead of the posh slums of Brentwood.

And if Zadie hadn't survived the Holocaust, none of us would be here in the first place.

Not quite true. Mom would be here, but the rest of us wouldn't.

"I think you can relax about all of this," Mom says. "They don't throw students out of private school."

"We signed a contract, Mom."

Mom's phone powers up and buzzes several times.

"How many calls . . . ?" Mom starts to say, and then looks at me. "You called me twenty-five times?"

I'm thinking I called Mom about five times. That means there are twenty or so calls from school. A couple dozen messages asking about her accident.

It's time to tell her what happened before I get in real trouble.

I'll tell her the truth and we can figure out how to

deal with the situation together. That's what parents and children are supposed to do. Problem solve. Talk it out.

"I only called you a few times," I tell Mom.

"Then who are all these people?" she says.

She holds the phone towards me like I'm going to decode it for her. Then she looks at it again.

She squints, trying to decide which message to listen to first.

I have to tell her now. It's always better to hear bad news from the source rather than second-hand. I know from experience. I learned about my parents' divorce when the process server handed Mom papers at the house one afternoon after I'd gotten home from school.

Mom starts to press her phone—

"Mom, when you didn't show up at school, I might have said something I shouldn't have—"

Mom tosses her phone on the table.

"I can't deal with this right now," she says.

It vibrates against the wood, another call coming in.

"It's too much. I need my music," Mom says, and heads for the living room.

I brace for an onslaught of yogic chanting. Mom puts it on every time she gets overwhelmed.

Her phone buzzes away on the table.

I turn it off.

I go into the living room. Mom is lying on a yoga mat on the floor, the chanting playing in the background.

Mom can practice yoga in the living room because we barely have any furniture. I have a bed, so I'm not exactly neglected, but if you want to relax in our house and you're not sleeping, you have to sit on a pillow on the floor. I'd kill for a soft chair. Cool leather that warms up when you sit in it for a while. If I told Mom I wanted a leather armchair, she'd accuse me of animal murder. But I figure you can make a leather chair out of a deceased cow. You don't have to kill it and steal its skin like Mom says. You just let it die peacefully and quietly, then you use it as a resource. Would the Great Spirit be angry about that?

Great Spirit. That's Mom's phrase.

Mom opens her eyes, her meditation ended.

"I'm back," she says. "Back and better than ever. Now, what did you want to tell me?"

"About tonight at school—"

"Sanskrit. I said I'm sorry I missed your conference. Can't we let bygones be bygones?"

"It isn't bygone. It's by-here."

Mom lifts her legs, presses with her hands, and effortlessly lifts herself up into a headstand.

Which leaves me looking at her butt.

"Mom. I'm trying to talk to you."

"I'm listening," she says.

"But you're upside down."

"Upside down is a matter of perspective. How do you know you're not the one who's upside down?"

"Because gravity is my friend right now. It's your enemy."

"It's both of our enemies. I'm just using it to my advantage."

This is our little game. Who is upside down, who is right side up? What's it all mean?

"I'm very upset—" I start to say.

"My son," Mom says, cutting me off.

It's formal and weird, but it does the trick. I'm a sucker for *my son*.

I take a step towards her.

Mom smiles at me from her headstand. People don't look the same upside down as they do right side up. Sometimes they look like monsters.

"Please don't be angry with me," Mom says. "I'll call school tomorrow and talk to them. I'll beg them for forgiveness. I'll get on my hands and knees—"

"It's not funny, Mom—"

"I'll tell them you're the best thing that's ever happened to them. The best thing that's happened to the Jewish race since sliced matzoh."

"We're not a race," I say.

"Whatever we are," Mom says.

"I don't want you to call," I say, because I can't have her calling school before I tell her what I did tonight. Then it occurs to me that maybe I don't have to tell her at all. I could just go into school and deal with the situation myself, leave Mom out of it entirely.

The more I think about it, the better the idea sounds to me.

"I'll take care of school," I say.

"Are you sure?" she says.

"Positive."

"Thank you, honey. Maybe you'll do a Dog with me before bed?"

Mom wants me to do the yoga pose Downward Facing Dog. I hate the Dog.

"Pretty please," she says.

I sigh, go down on all fours.

"Now tuck into a crouch," Mom says, going into teacher mode.

I tuck, but I feel my body fighting me. My head would like to do what Mom wants, but my flesh resists. It doesn't like being folded up. It wants to expand. It wants to breathe freely.

"Can you roll over and up?" Mom says.

I try, but I don't have enough strength in my core. That's what Mom calls your middle section.

"Sorry," I say, after I fall twice.

"It's okay, honey," Mom says. "You'll get it eventually. It's not about perfection. It's about the fact that we keep trying."

She's making an effort to sound patient, but I hear the frustration. Mom's a yoga teacher. She should be able to teach her son yoga.

"Do a modified," she says.

I do a modified headstand, first leaning forward, then climbing my feet up the back of the wall behind me. When I'm nearly upside down, Mom says:

"I have to tell you what happened tonight at the Center."

Mom works at the Center for Yogic Expression in Brentwood. It's more than a yoga studio. It's a movement. A community. A way of life. Forty other things, too, at least according to their brochure.

"It's so exciting," Mom says. "Maybe you'll understand why I forgot about your conference."

I doubt it, I think. Then I say, "Tell me everything, Mom."

That earns me a huge smile. Mom loves it when she's the center of attention.

"We had our monthly meeting, and they asked me to teach a prenatal class!" Mom says. "Can you believe it?"

"Is that good?"

"It's amazing. So many things are coming towards me right now—in my personal life, at work. I'm very open to receiving gifts from the universe."

"What's happening in your personal life?" I crane my neck to look at Mom from the headstand.

"If I told you, it wouldn't be personal," she says with a wink.

Does Mom have a new boyfriend? The idea makes my stomach turn. Mom isn't known for her primo choices when it comes to love. Every few months she crashes and burns with some loser, and Sweet Caroline and I are left to pick up the pieces.

"I want to tell you about the prenatal class," Mom says. "I finally get to share my maternal experience *and* my yoga training. Mommies and babies in a class, Sanskrit. How exciting is that?"

"If it's prenatal, they're not babies yet."

"They're still babies. They're just interior babies."

"There's no such thing, Mom."

"I don't mean it literally. I mean life, Sanskrit. They are alive in there, and I can get them started on yoga at a critical time in their development."

"They'll be born doing Salute to the Placenta."

"That's funny, sweetie, but I'm serious about this. You can affect a child in a very positive way if you intervene early. I wish I'd known about yoga before you were born."

Mom didn't become a yoga freak until after the divorce. Does she think there's something wrong with me that yoga would have made better?

"Is that your big news?" I say. "That's why you missed my conference?"

"It's only the first part," she says, "and part two is the best part, because it's about you."

"What about me?"

"I need your help to teach the class."

"I can't teach yoga. I can't even do yoga."

"You don't have to teach. I want the ladies to see us together, see how we interact as mother and son."

"Why me? Why not Sweet Caroline?"

"Sweet Caroline hates yoga. Besides, she's busy with her friends."

"And I'm not?"

"You've got more free time. Anyway, I want the ladies to see what it's like to have a boy."

"What's it like?"

"What kind of question is that?"

The weirder a conversation gets with Mom, the more she acts like everything she's saying is obvious and you're an idiot for not getting it.

"So you want me to help you teach a prenatal yoga class?"

"Not want. I *need* you," Mom says. "I can't do it without you."

That makes me feel good, even if it is crazy.

"The first class is tomorrow afternoon. We could go to dinner after," Mom says. "We can break my juice fast together."

"Just you and me?"

"You, me, delicious food, and an adjacent bathroom."

"Too much information," I say, and Mom laughs.

I try to remember the last time Mom and I did something like that. I don't come up with anything.

"Does that sound good?" Mom says.

"I'll check my schedule. Yup, I'm free," I say.

"Sanskrit," she says, and she smiles.

Just my name and a smile. Nothing else.

I feel dizzy from it. Or maybe it's the headstand.

I think about school and everything that happened earlier tonight. I try to feel how angry I was, but I can't right now.

"I knew I could count on you," Mom says. She effortlessly drops out of her headstand.

"Bathroom again," she says, and she scurries off, her bare feet slapping on the wood floor.

I drop out of my headstand, and I get the spins. I close my eyes, get down on all fours like an animal.

I wait for the world to stop moving.

For a second I think it's not going to happen, I'm going to be in permanent spin, a comet spiraling forever in the darkness of space.

Then my head slows, the nausea passes, and the room comes back to stillness.

I'm not lost in space. I'm in our living room without any chairs.

"It was a snowball rolling down a hill."

That's what Herschel says a few minutes later when I call him from my room. I have to keep my voice down because Mom hates for me to use the cell phone when I'm in the house. She hates for me to use it at all. She's afraid the radiation will affect my brain. For similar reasons, she won't buy me a laptop because she doesn't want me to put it on my lap in case I want to have kids in the future. It's crazy.

"I was hoping the teachers would be discreet," I say.

"They were discreet. They discreetly announced to everyone that you were in the midst of a major family crisis and could use the support of the community."

"That's discretion?"

"*Jewish* discretion. Did you get a lot of calls after that?"

"Not as many as you would have gotten."

"What's that mean?"

"Come on, Herschel. The community loves you. What happened when you broke your foot?"

"People were very supportive, thank God."

"You said you got two hundred calls."

"More like a hundred. But this is not a competition."

"Of course not."

"How many did you get?" Herschel says.

"Eighteen."

"Eighteen." Herschel pauses, searching for the right thing to say. "That's not insignificant."

"It's not a hundred."

"It's only one night, and only the junior class knows. Wait until tomorrow."

I think about the entire school hearing the story of my mother's accident.

Herschel says, "Not that there will be a tomorrow. You're going to set the record straight, aren't you?"

"I can't. Mom doesn't know what happened."

Silence on the line.

"I tried to tell her. It's just . . . It's complicated, Herschel."

"The longer this goes on, the worse it will be."

I pace in my room, run my finger over the collection of Talmud on my shelf. My finger comes away covered in dust.

"What am I going to do?" I say.

"Are you asking me for advice?" Herschel says.

"Yes."

"I won't give it to you."

"Don't play this game now. I can't take it."

"No game. It's not my job to tell you what to do," Herschel says. "I've made that mistake before and I've learned my lesson."

"Then give me spiritual counseling," I say.

When Herschel tries to counsel me, I usually slap him down, remind him he's not a rabbi but a seventeen-year-old kid who started wearing *payis* two years ago. But right now I keep quiet.

"The Torah teaches us that if you tell a lie, you become a liar," Herschel says. "It's a matter of character."

"But there are extenuating circumstances. I mean, one lie in and of itself does not make me a liar, right?"

"If you commit one murder, you are a murderer. Why would a lie be any different?"

"Because nobody died from my lie."

"Your soul died a little."

"Oh, please."

"You don't think so?" Herschel says.

"What if I had lied to the Nazis?"

"There are no Nazis."

"But there were. Follow my logic."

"Lied about what?" he says.

"Let's say I was in Poland during the war, and the Nazis asked where my family was hiding, and I lied to them."

"It's still a lie," Herschel says. "But I think God might forgive a lie that's intended to save a life."

"This is similar."

"How so?"

"It's a lie to save my college career."

"College is not equivalent to a human life."

"Brandeis is."

"Very funny."

"So you want me to tell the professors the truth? What about Yitzhak?"

Yitzhak was a visiting Israeli student who broke the Code of Conduct last year. He got expelled for plagiarism.

"They sent him all the way back to Tel Aviv," I say.

"Actions have consequences," Herschel says. "I know better than most."

"Please. When have you ever been in trouble?"

Herschel clears his throat. "Don't change the subject. We're talking about you. And ethics."

I groan. Where is the old Herschel who used to give advice? That's what friends do for other friends. They tell you what you should do when you're in a bind and can't decide for yourself. But Herschel has become some sort of sage who speaks in abstractions and biblical verses. It's frustrating.

"It's late now," Herschel says. "Sleep on it, pray on it, and you'll know the right answer in the morning."

Thanks for nothing, I think.

But I don't say it. I express my gratitude, hang up, and turn off the phone.

Pray on it.

What does that really mean? I can say the Hebrew prayers they teach me in school, but they have no meaning to me. I can use the English translations, but those just sound like gibberish. They all begin the same way:

Blessed art thou, O Lord our God, King of the universe . . .

I sit on my bed. I think about all the different prayers I know.

Dr. Prem, the chiropractor that Mom sends me to, calls out to the Divine.

"Repeat after me," he says. "I am willing, ready, and able to experience the Divine."

But I'm not willing, ready, and able.

Mom tells me to access the Great Spirit.

None of those works for me.

I should be praying to *HaShem*. That's what they teach us.

I try it in my own words. I say, "I'm sorry, *HaShem*, for lying about Mom—"

I can't even finish the prayer. I feel like an idiot, alone and talking to myself in an empty room.

Is this what prayer is supposed to feel like?

Instead of praying, I get practical. I need to buy myself some time. But how?

Mom's phone.

I open my door and slip into the hallway.

Mom and Sweet Caroline are in bed.

I make my way to the kitchen.

I navigate by moonlight shining through the kitchen window. I can see the black square of Mom's phone still on the kitchen table where she tossed it. She often leaves it on the table and forgets to plug it in. Then she's baffled when it's not charged the next day. Usually I plug it in for her, but that has the unintended effect of making her believe there are power fairies who keep her battery at 100 percent.

I pick up the phone, slip it into my pocket—

"What are you doing?" Sweet Caroline says.

She's standing in the kitchen doorway. I swear, the girl has elephant ears.

"Nothing," I whisper.

"You're taking Mom's phone."

"I'm plugging it in for her."

"The plug is on the counter. You're putting it in your pocket."

"Jesus."

"Don't take the Lord's name in vain."

"He's not our Lord."

"He's someone's Lord. You could have a little respect for that."

"Not now, Caroline."

She sucks in a quick breath. Her cheeks puff

out, and she picks at the corner of her lip.

"Don't pick," I say. She picks until she bleeds. It's as gross as it sounds.

"Don't tell me what to do!" she says. She pulls on her lip even harder.

"*Sweet* Caroline," I say quickly. "Very sweet."

She relaxes a little and comes into the kitchen.

"Why are you stealing Mom's phone?"

"I'm prepping it for her. For the morning. She asked me to."

"So I can tell her you're doing it?"

"Tell her whatever you want," I say.

"I will. First thing in the morning."

She starts to leave.

"Wait—"

"What?"

"I'm stealing Mom's phone," I say.

"Why?"

"I'm in trouble."

That perks her up. Sweet Caroline loves trouble. Especially other people's.

"What kind of trouble?" she says.

"The kind that gets you thrown out of school."

"That's not a problem."

"Why not?"

"You hate school."

"I can't get expelled. I have to do college applications in a few months. How can I explain something like that?"

"You can always do a year in Israel. They'll take anyone."

"Very funny," I say.

Sweet Caroline hops onto a chair at the kitchen counter.

"So, what happened?" she says.

"It's a secret."

"I love secrets."

"You can't tell anyone."

"Of course not," she says. "But how can I keep a secret if I don't know what the secret is?"

Before I open my mouth, I know it's a mistake.

It's always a mistake to tell secrets to Sweet Caroline. It's like the Miranda warnings. Anything you say may be used against you. Only in Sweet Caroline's case, it *will* be used against you. But how can I keep this secret without her help?

I know I shouldn't say anything.

But I do.

"You're in trouble, Sanskrit."

I open my eyes. Mom is standing outside my room with my door cracked open. We don't open each other's doors in our house without permission. It's part of Mom's respect-the-individual policy.

I sit up, panicked.

"What kind of trouble?" I say. I'm imagining all manner of terrible things. Sweet Caroline ratted me out. Professors from school came to the door.

"You're late for school," Mom says through the tiny crack.

Most mothers wake you up *before* you're late for school. At least this is what I've been told.

"You overslept," Mom says. "Sorry."

The clock says 8:15. I sit up in bed.

"Will you drive us?" I say.

"Sweet Caroline already left. You know how she is."

Right. Sweet Caroline sets two alarms, then wakes

up before both of them. It's the definition of anal adolescence.

"She didn't bother to wake us up?" I say.

Mom shrugs. Sweet Caroline's still a perfect little
girl in her eyes. A perfect little girl who goes to a
psychologist. But we're not supposed to talk about
that.

"Of course I'll drive you. Just let me hop in the
shower."

Mom closes my door.

That's when it hits me. Mom can't drive me because
the school thinks she was in a car accident. If we pull
up smiling and waving, it's going to be a disaster.

"Mom!" I shout.

I jump out of bed. The air is cool on my bare legs. I
catch sight of myself in the mirror. I see a scrawny kid,
a miniature version of Dad. I think of Dad crammed
into his home workshop surrounded by clutter. The
last time he had a date was the middle of the last
decade. That does not bode well for my future.

"Mom!"

I hear the shower running in the bathroom down
the hall.

I rush back into my room and slide on yesterday's
jeans. Choosing clothes is hard enough on a good day.
On a bad day it's better to just sniff yesterday's pants
and put them back on. Fewer decisions. Less room for
error.

The pocket is heavy. I reach in and pull out Mom's phone.

Last night comes rushing back to me.

I make sure Mom is still in the shower, and I turn on the phone. It takes a minute to warm up, and then the NEW VOICE MAIL window starts to pop.

"Did you call me?" Mom says. She's suddenly in my door, dripping wet in a towel.

I jam her phone into my pocket. The e-mail indicator chimes.

"What's that?" she says.

"Nothing," I say. "Hey, Mom, forget the ride. I'm going to walk with Herschel this morning instead."

"You never walk with him anymore."

"That's not true," I say, even though it is.

"Hasn't school already—"

"I just called him. He's late, too," I say. "Funny coincidence."

"Alright then. I have to run. I've got a level I-II at 8:30 and I can't be late."

"Good luck."

"Don't forget our prenatal class this afternoon."

"I'm there. I promise," I say.

And unlike Mom, I keep my promises.

Mom smiles and pats at her thigh with the corner of the towel.

"By the way, have you seen my phone?"

"Haven't seen it," I say.

Mom shrugs and disappears down the hall. Five minutes later she's out the door, and I've got a choice to make. Do I go to school and lie all day? Or do I lie once and stay home?

I decide to risk it at school.

"The universe is not what we think it is."

That's what Professor Schwartzburg says in the middle of English class that afternoon. Then he pauses as good teachers do, waiting to see if he's hooked us.

He hasn't. It's English class. Why is he talking about the universe again?

We hate him for this.

Or maybe it's just me.

I'm in a terrible mood from dodging questions about Mom all day. Herschel wasn't kidding about the school community leaping into action. Everyone is worried. Everyone is asking about our family. Each question has put me in a progressively fouler mood and forced me to lie more. My usual patience with Schwartzburg's philosophical musings is hanging by a thread.

"There is a great, mysterious force out there," Professor Schwartzburg says. He adjusts his sports coat, yanking it down by the flaps.

"What we thought was the fabric of the universe is not the fabric at all," he says. "There is something greater underneath—a force that has been there all along, but has been invisible to us until recently."

He fails to mention there is a great, mysterious force in here, sitting four rows in front of me. It is in the form of a girl.

Not just any girl.

The Initials.

It's hard to ignore her when I see her every day in Schwartzburg's class. Four rows. That's all that separates us. That means I'm treated to an exquisite view of the back of her head, her left earlobe, the flip of hair when she uses her finger to push it behind said earlobe, the left shoulder upon which the hair falls, and sometimes, if only for a second, the side of her face as she turns to whisper to Talya Stein. I watch her lips moving from four rows away and try to guess what she's saying. I imagine I am Talya Stein's ear and The Initials' words are for me, each one carried on a puff of sweet breath.

"You will not find this force in our physics or astronomy textbooks," Professor Schwartzburg says. "Scientists have only begun to understand it. They call it *dark matter*."

The Initials twists a flap of hair, spinning her finger around and around.

She might as well be spinning me.

The Initials is my great burden to bear. I have to see her each day, all the while knowing we will never be closer than we were in second grade. Our glory days have been over for almost as long as my sister has been alive.

If that isn't a powerful force, I don't know what is.

"Excuse me, professor," Herschel says. "What does any of this have to do with *Gatsby*?"

We've been reading *The Great Gatsby*, which I've taken to calling *The Great Goyim* when Herschel and I are alone.

"What does anything have to do with anything?" Professor Schwartzburg says.

Herschel shakes his head, and his *payis,* the little curls that religious Jews wear in front of their ears, jiggle back and forth. Herschel is the only one who lets his *payis* grow in our school. He's the most Jewish kid in Jewish school, and I am the least. Although my family is technically Jewish, without Zadie's money I would never be in religious school. We're like a lot of families in Los Angeles. Not seriously Jewish. More like Jewish adjacent.

Herschel's family used to be just like us. They pushed him into Jewish school solely for the academics, and he hated it as much as I did. He lives down the street, and we'd walk to school every day bad-mouthing the hell out of the place.

Then Herschel went on a school trip to Israel along with most of the freshman class. He tried to get me to come along, but I told him the Jews spent forty years wandering lost in the desert. Why should we volunteer to go back?

Something happened to Herschel on that trip. When he returned, he took a cab directly from LAX to my house. I opened the door to find a bearded kid in a black suit and a fedora.

"Herschel? Is that you?" I said.

"We've got it all wrong, Sanskrit."

"What do we have wrong?" I said.

"God. Judaism. It's not what we thought it was."

"What is it?" I said.

"It's . . . life or death," he said. "We have to find God. It's our true purpose in this world."

That's when I knew I'd lost him. He left L.A. as my best friend and returned as Zero Mostel in *Fiddler on the Roof*. Sometimes kids get flipped liked Herschel, but a few weeks of L.A. traffic and In-N-Out Burger help them come to their senses. But it's been nearly two years since that trip, and the old Herschel is nowhere to be seen.

Now that Herschel is a super Jew, I'm all alone at the bottom of the religious pack, slightly below Tyler, who's only Jewish on his mother's side. He's part of the executive committee's diversity initiative. Actually, he's the entire diversity initiative. They tried to recruit a few non-observant Jews when the economy slumped, but none of them lasted except him. It turns out that not a lot of non-observant Jews want to observe. Big surprise.

"Professor, I want to read *Gatsby*," Tyler says. I notice he's been paying close attention since we started reading the book. Something about Gatsby's search for identity is very moving to him.

"*Gatsby* is all of us," Professor Schwartzburg says, seeming to get his lecture back on course. "Just as this mysterious dark matter winds its way through everything."

So much for back on track.

"I agree with Tyler," I say, trying to score some points. "I'd like to get back to the novel."

I'm hoping The Initials will turn around and see who said it, but she doesn't. Back of her head. That's all I get. Eight months of rear view. While it's not a terrible sight, it's only half of what I want.

"We will return to the novel, of course," Professor Schwartzburg says. "By the way, how is your mother, Aaron?"

Another teacher who won't use my first name.

"I'm waiting for word," I say.

"Keep your cell phone on," Schwartzburg says, which is against school policy, but overnight I've become the guy who gets special treatment.

"Oh, it's on," I say.

"We're here for you," Barry Goldwasser says to me.

I hate Barry Goldwasser.

He's the founder of the Mitzvah Minute Club, our school service organization. Their mission statement? *Good deeds in under a minute.*

They only do mitzvahs that can be done in under a minute. On one level it's genius. You pick up a piece of trash, you help an old lady across the street, you offer a dollar to a homeless man. It doesn't cost you much in terms of time, money, or effort. Goodness is spread across the barren and selfish landscape that is Los Angeles, one sixty-second burst at a time.

But if you think about it, you realize it's total crap. What if I need ninety seconds of help? I can't call the Mitzvah boys? If you're going to help people, then help. Don't put a time limit on it. That's something my mother would do.

"Aaron, I hope you will lean on *HaShem*," Professor Schwartzburg says. "What else can we do in these trying times?"

I can think of a lot of things we can do, but I keep them to myself.

Schwartzburg sighs and leans back against the whiteboard.

"*HaShem*," he says, and clutches his chest.

The class leans forward. Either he's having a spiritual experience or a heart attack. Stories of dark matter may not get our attention, but the potential stirrings of a heart attack do, especially after losing two professors to myocardial infarction in the last year.

"Are you in the heart attack pool?" I whisper to Herschel.

"That's disgusting," he says.

"I'm just saying Schwartzburg doesn't look good."

Herschel shakes his head. He's too pious for a heart attack pool. I can't really blame him.

Barry Goldwasser jumps up. He's obviously not in the pool either.

"Are you alright, professor?" he says.

Just my luck. Barry is going to save Schwartzburg from a heart attack in under a minute, and he's going to do it right in front of The Initials. He'll become the hero of the junior class, and I'll fade a little further into obscurity.

But Schwartzburg pulls himself back from the brink. He stands and brushes himself off. "Sorry. This situation with Aaron's family has me flustered," Schwartzburg says.

"It has us all upset," Barry Goldwasser says. "We should do something for them."

The students nod in agreement.

Barry looks at me, his face full of kindness and pity. I want to punch him.

The end-of-class tone rings through the school. Another English class is over without our having discussed English.

The Initials stands up. I look at the outline of her butt beneath the long skirt. Does she have on bicycle shorts, regular shorts, or leggings today? She bends over to get her books. I decide it's probably leggings. And under the leggings?

"Hello?" Herschel says.

"I'm sorry. Did you say something?"

"I said that maybe I should talk to Schwartzburg. He seems upset lately. He's lectured about dark matter three times this week."

"Don't talk to him."

"He might need an ear."

"He doesn't need an ear. He needs an antidepressant."

"You never want to get involved, Sanskrit. That's not service. *HaShem* would have us be of service."

"I've got enough problems. I can't take on God's problems, too. If *HaShem* is all-powerful, why does he need my help?"

Herschel looks at me with that pitying look on his face. He not only found God in Israel; he found superiority.

The class shuffles out of the room. I notice Barry Goldwasser falls in next to The Initials.

"I saw you davening this morning," he says. "Very nice."

Davening. That's what we do during the mandatory morning prayer service—rock back and forth as we talk to *HaShem*. I like to sneak peeks at The Initials davening through the divider that separates the guys and girls while we're praying. She really gets into it, her eyes closed, her breath coming in little gasps.

"You shouldn't be watching the girls during prayer," The Initials says.

"Not the girls," Barry says. "Just you."

The Initials smiles.

Ugh. Another reason to hate Barry.

For the next few days, most of the school will be praying for the Zuckermans, asking God to help my mother, asking him to be with my family as we struggle through this trying time.

And me?

I'll be thinking about other things like I always do during prayers.

Nobody would confuse me with a religious kid. That's because I hate B-Jew, and I'm not exactly subtle about it. Not everyone loves the religious part of school, but even the most cynical of them can admit we've got great academics, a cool faculty, lots of extra-curriculars.

None of that matters to me. I just feel trapped.

It's because I never chose this place. It was chosen for me.

For that, I can thank my grandfather, Zadie Zuckerman.

"Your grandpa was a real mamzer bastard."

That's what my father said one day when I was ten years old. We were in Roxbury Park watching the lawn bowling tournament. It's a Los Angeles tradition. Old men dress in white and lawn bowl in the middle of Beverly Hills. I guess the men reminded my father of Abe Zuckerman, my grandfather who we called Zadie. He had died a few weeks before. My father cried like a baby at his funeral, but the minute it was over he seemed fine, even happy.

"Your zadie was a tough old bastard," Dad said. "A real survivor."

"I know," I say, but I didn't know much. We weren't allowed to ask about the war, and Zadie hardly ever mentioned it. He always wore long-sleeve shirts to cover the number tattooed on his forearm when he was twelve years old.

"I've got something to tell you about your zadie,"

my father said. "There's good news and bad news."

"Good news first," I said.

I was ten, but I was no idiot.

"The good news is that your grandfather had some money. In fact a good deal of money. You know your zadie was in the *shmata* business."

"Terry cloth," I said.

"That's right," Dad said. "The West Coast king of terry."

I knew this because I had more bathrobes than any kid I'd ever met.

"Terry bought us our house," Dad said. "And it made a very nice life for your zadie."

I started to get excited. "Are we rich?" I said, because plenty of ten-year-olds in Brentwood had cell phones then, and I didn't have one. No cell phone, no new clothes, but more fuzzy towels than the Beverly Hills Hotel.

"We are not rich," Dad says. "A long way from it. But you, son, are in good shape. Your zadie put money in a trust for you."

As it turns out, that was the bad news.

"Now let me tell you why your grandfather was a mamzer bastard," my father said.

Calling someone a mamzer bastard is a little redundant, like calling them a "bastard bastard," which doesn't make a lot of sense. But that's exactly what my father said. I remember very well.

"Why was he a mamzer?" I asked.

"Your trust has restrictions," my father said.

"What kind of restrictions?"

"You must use it to get an education."

"An education is good, right?"

"A *Jewish* education," my father said.

"What does that mean?" I said.

"It means you've got a lot of Hebrew school in front of you, my boy."

I'd been going to Hebrew school for three hours every Saturday—three of the longest hours of my life. My parents were still married then, and they went to Shabbat services on Saturday mornings to keep Zadie happy. They'd drop us off at Hebrew school beforehand along with the rest of the parents. We'd sit in a circle on the cold linoleum floor singing Jewish songs and being told to *sheket bevakasha* when we couldn't keep quiet.

If Hebrew school was bad at three hours, what was Jewish school every day going to be like?

"What if I don't want a Jewish education?" I said to Dad.

"If you don't want a Jewish education, you don't get the money," my father said. "And your mother and I are royally screwed when it comes to tuition payments."

"But it's not like the money goes away. It's still there, right?"

"It's there, but it's not for you."

"Who is it for?"

"Tay-Sachs," my father said. "It's a Jewish disease."

That's got me worried. I had Jewish genes. We all did.

"Do I have Tay-Sachs?" I said.

"You do not have Tay-Sachs," my father said. "Certainly not. But if you don't go to Jewish school, your money goes for Tay-Sachs research."

"So, it's me or Tay-Sachs," I said.

"That's right. Your zadie wants to save all the Jews, and he doesn't mind screwing his own family in the process."

I didn't like the sound of that.

"There's no free ride in this world," my father said. "People always want something from you, Sanskrit. I learned my lesson living with your zadie. Every time you rub your tushy with a soft towel in this family, you lose a little part of yourself."

My grandfather was a mamzer bastard. That proved it.

"They're girls, not gods."

Herschel interrupts me while I'm staring at The Initials in the downstairs hallway. She's bending over and taking books out of her cabinet. That's what they call lockers in my school. As if changing the word could change the fact that it's still a door with a lock on it.

I try to look away from her, but I can't. Or maybe I don't want to. Maybe I like to suffer.

"Did you hear me?" Herschel says.

I manage to shift my eyes from The Initials to Herschel. It's not a great trade-off. His head is covered with his favorite oversized black felt yarmulke, a billboard for the devout.

"We all have our loves," I say. "I have girls. You have the Holy Land."

"That's apples and oranges," Herschel says.

"Or grapefruits in her case," I say.

Herschel scowls. He used to like talking about girls'

breasts. Now a little fruit metaphor sends him over the edge.

"The way you look at them. It's not right."

"How do I look at them?"

"Like you're seeing *HaShem*."

"They're as close to *HaShem* as I get," I say.

Herschel is accusing me of elevating girls to the level of God. This would be the ultimate in sacrilege, like worshipping golden idols or slaughtering the fatted calf.

"They're people like us," Herschel says. "They make mistakes, they struggle."

"How would you know?" I say.

Herschel hasn't had a single girlfriend in high school, and since getting back from Israel, he hasn't wanted one.

"I'm reminding you that Judi is just a girl," Herschel says.

"Please don't use her name," I say, interrupting him.

Because I don't want to hear it. I don't even want to hear the syllables come together. Syllables form sounds, sounds create meaning, meaning coalesces into a name—

And this name has the power to destroy me.

A name should not have so much power. Herschel is right about that.

There are other girls in school, cute girls. I get mini crushes from time to time—an Israeli exchange student passes through or one of the hot girls suddenly gets rebellious and hikes her skirt up an extra inch—but the crushes never last.

Nobody is like The Initials.

That's why I protect myself from the name. I don't want to hear it, and I never say it.

Maybe then I won't think of her so much.

Maybe then I can forget.

"You think you're number one, but you're not."

She bit her lip when she said it. Bit and then licked to soothe the bite, her fists balling up to challenge me.

This is The Initials in second grade. Back when she was just Judi Jacobs. JJ. An annoying girl in my second grade class.

She walked up and challenged me, and we'd barely ever spoken before.

"I'm the best speller in school," I said. "Now and always."

"Not anymore," she said. "I'm going to win the spelling bee this week."

I laughed in her face. Her ugly, freckled face.

We weren't in Jewish school then. Zadie wanted my parents to enroll me, but they'd resisted. My mother in particular. She was playing along with being Jewish, but the façade was cracking. She was starting to push back on Zadie. So Judi and I were in public school in

Brentwood, where we were fighting to be at the top of the class.

I looked Judi in the eye. I could still do that then. I was brave.

"You suck at spelling," I said, which wasn't technically true. "So I'm not worried."

"You only got a ninety-six on the quiz last week," she said.

"I blew one word. Big deal."

I didn't question how she knew my score or think about why she was paying attention to me. I took it for granted. How would I have behaved if I'd known it was the Golden Age, and Judi would spend the next eight years ignoring me? She would ignore me in public school, then ignore me even more when we ended up at B-Jew together.

She lifted her arms and flexed her muscles like a weight lifter. If she did that today, I would look at her chest. Pray for the cotton to stretch. Look for the curves beneath her oversized sweater.

But I didn't look at chests then. I looked girls in the eye. And I hated them. Most of them.

Judi Jacobs in particular.

"We'll see who's best at the bee tomorrow," she said.

"Yes, we will," I said.

"JJ!" her friend called her.

I walked away, silently hating her, actively planning her demise. I wanted to see Judi Jacobs suffer. I wanted her to be ashamed in front of the entire class.

I went home and studied extra hard that night, memorizing every word, making sure I knew the pronunciation and the origin, paying special attention to silent letters that might trip me up.

I woke up the next morning feeling strong and happy, ready to crush her in the spelling bee.

How could I have known that was the beginning of the end?

"This is a trial, but it will pass."

That's what the dean says after cornering Herschel and me in the hall. I tell him things have been touch and go with my mom. He stands there looking at me and shaking his head, and I have to pretend I'm really upset. I'm not good at acting, but luckily I've got plenty of real things to be upset about. Most of them female.

"I could barely sleep last night," the dean says. "Your mother wasn't answering her phone."

Herschel gives me a look. It's too much for me. The lying, the silent scorn from Herschel, everyone treating me so nicely.

"I have to tell you something, dean," I say.

"Aaron," he says. He puts a hand on my shoulder. "I've been hard on you this year. The academic probation. The family contract with your mother. You think I'm out to get you, I know, but it's not the truth. It's because I believe in you. In your potential."

I step back, subtly shrugging off his hand.

"I appreciate that, sir," I say.

"Now this has happened," the dean says. "I don't want you to worry so much about school. Let us carry you for a while."

Being carried. It sounds nice. I think of a prince being held aloft on a platform covered with soft pillows. Prince Sanskrit.

Herschel clears his throat.

"You wanted to tell me something?" the dean says.

"No. I mean, there's nothing to tell yet. We're still waiting to hear from the doctor," I say.

"Is she at Cedars?" the dean says. "I'd like to come by and offer my support."

It didn't occur to me that people would want to visit her. I hadn't thought that far in advance. Now I need a story that will keep them away.

"She was at a yoga conference in Orange County when it happened," I say.

Orange County. The foreign land thirty miles south of us.

The dean whistles through his teeth. No way he wants to drive to Orange County. At least that's what I'm hoping.

"How terrible," the dean says. "When will she be back?"

"That's the problem," I say. "We're trying to get her

home, but she can't be moved yet. I think they're going to rehabilitate her down there."

"That will be expensive," the dean says.

I lower my head. I'm learning that if I don't have a good answer, I can just look at the ground. This doesn't work under normal circumstances—in class, for instance, when a teacher asks me a question—but during a tragedy, people don't seem to mind it.

"It's going to be okay," the dean says.

"I know it will," I say, my head still down.

"In the meantime, we'd like to send a basket. Something to let her know the community is thinking about her."

"You could send it to the house. I'll make sure she gets it," I say. And then I add, "Mom loves chocolate."

Which is an outright lie. Mom doesn't eat sugar at all. But if we're going to start getting gift baskets, why not go for something good?

"That's what we'll do," the dean says. His voice turns hyperserious: "If you need anything. Absolutely anything. Do not hesitate."

I'm having bad thoughts, like using the situation to get out of doing homework, but I squelch the idea. This is going to blow up in my face at some point. Why make it worse?

"I will not hesitate," I say, as seriously as I can.

"Don't."

"I won't."

"Thatta boy," he says, and he goes down the hall.

Herschel shakes his head. "Rehabilitation? Where did you get that from?"

"I had to say something. If they think Mom is at Cedars Sinai, they're going to want to see her."

"You're lying to the man's face."

"I'll tell the truth eventually."

"When?"

"I just need some time to work it out," I say.

Just then the CORE crew passes by, the hardcore religious kids. The administration hand selected a group of particularly devout students last year and put them in an accelerated religious studies program. They even daven in a separate room every morning, personally coached by the rabbi.

"*Boker tov*," one of the guys shouts to Herschel.

Why can't he just say *good morning* like everyone else? You don't have to prove you speak Hebrew. Everyone in the damn school speaks Hebrew.

Herschel waves.

"I have to catch up to my boys," he says. "Do the right thing, huh?"

"Of course," I say.

"Yo, yo, yo! *Shalom chaverim!*" Herschel shouts to the guys, and they head down the hall together.

I turn around to see if The Initials is still there, and Tyler is at the cabinet next to mine. He's clutching a religious studies textbook like a life preserver.

"I'm praying for your mom," he says.

"Which prayer?" I say.

"What?"

"Which prayer specifically are you saying?"

Tyler looks flustered. I'm being a jerk, but I can't help it.

He says, "It's not—I don't mean a specific prayer. I mean prayer in general."

Tyler motions for me to come closer. He leans towards me, lowering his voice to a whisper.

"If you want to know the truth, I believe he'll help you," he says. He points to the ceiling.

"Who?"

"Jesus."

"I thought you were Jewish," I say.

"Half-Jewish. Half other things."

"Isn't that confusing?"

"Not really. It's all God," he says.

"You're killing me. I'm dying."

That's what Sweet Caroline says on the phone. She never calls in the middle of the day—or any time of day for that matter. That's why I pick up. I excuse myself from math class by holding up my phone, and then I take the call out in the hall.

Tragedy has its privileges.

"How am I killing you?" I whisper.

"Do you know what it's like here—"

"Wait a minute, how are you calling me? You can't have cell phones in school."

"I'm in the bathroom," she says, "and I smuggled my phone in."

I sometimes forget that Sweet Caroline has it even worse than me. She's at a superstrict all-girls Jewish school. At least my school is coed so there's something to look at besides the Torah.

"They're asking about Mom," she says.

"How is that possible? You don't even go to my school."

"It's Jewish geography, like Dad says. They all talk."

"Who's asking?" I say.

"The head of school. The teachers. Everyone."

"Crap," I say. "How bad is it?"

"They want to know what they can do, how they can help, how I'm holding up. You know the deal."

"What did you tell them?"

"I told them to send a gift basket to the house."

I laugh.

"What's so funny?"

"Great minds think alike," I say, even though I never considered Sweet Caroline to be in that particular club.

"It's not funny, Sanskrit. I have to walk around looking sad all day, and it doesn't come naturally. I'm a happy kid."

A happy kid with a psychologist. But I don't say that.

I say, "If it helps at all, I told them Mom is at a hospital in Orange County. So nobody can come to visit her."

"You're making my life miserable, and I don't appreciate it."

"I'm sorry. I didn't think it would get out of school."

"How sorry are you?"

"What does that mean?"

"Are you twenty dollars sorry?"

"Goddamn you—"

"Lord's name—" she says.

I stop myself. Not because I don't want to take the Lord's name in vain, but because if I go off on Sweet Caroline right now, I could be in big trouble.

"Twenty dollars?" I say.

"A week."

"I don't have that kind of money."

"It should be more," she says. "But we'll start with twenty. Remember, I'm keeping the secret, too."

I think about ways to come up with twenty dollars a week. I'll have to break into my book fund.

"Deal," I say. Anything to keep Sweet Caroline on board.

"I can lie for a while," she says, "but Mom better have a spontaneous recovery before Passover. We're supposed to show up for the seder, right?"

Passover. Next week.

"I'll take care of it," I say.

I hear the toilet flush over the phone.

"Were you peeing while you were talking to me?" I say.

"I'm multitasking," she says, and hangs up.

"I've got a little situation, professor."

That's all I have to say when I go back into math class.
I don't even walk all the way in, just stick my head in
the door and hold up the phone.

"Of course," the professor says, waving me off. "I'll
let your other professors know."

I feel a little guilty ending school at one o'clock,
but I've got business to attend to. Sweet Caroline's
report has me worried, and I want to get back to the
house.

I walk through school in the middle of the day, all
alone in the main hallway. I feel free, like the rules
don't apply to me anymore. I could walk into any
room right now. I could interrupt Herschel's science
class and say I need him, pull him out. I could ask for
a meeting with the dean. I could do anything.

I feel good, I feel powerful.

But as soon as I get outside, I start to feel bad again.
I rush through Brentwood with my head down, afraid

someone from Mom's yoga studio will see me. Would Mom even care if she knew I was walking around in the middle of the day? I could make some lame excuse and she'd believe me. You can tell Mom just about anything, and she'll buy it. That's because you have to pay attention to notice a lie, and then you have to be willing to do something about it if you do. Mom doesn't qualify in either category.

But even she would freak out if she knew I was telling people she was in an accident. And if I got thrown out of school, I don't know what we would do. How would we pay for college if not with Zadie's money? Forget Brandeis. I'd be taking the bus to Santa Monica Community College every day.

When I get home, I go into my room and take Mom's phone from under my mattress. When I turn it on, she's up to thirty-eight messages. I need to make the phone disappear.

I could just put it in a closet, but Mom might be smart enough to use the Find My Phone app, or find someone smart enough to do it for her. That means I have to do away with the phone for good.

I pop out the SIM card and snap it in half.

Then I think about Sweet Caroline. I can't trust her to do the right thing, even for twenty dollars. I need some leverage.

I head down the hall to her room. If she finds out I went into her room without permission, there will be hell to pay. Not that I want to spend much time in her room. It looks like the Disney Store threw up in there.

I check around her doorframe for traps. Sure enough, there's a piece of string near the bottom of the door-jamb. If you open it, the string falls out. Then she knows someone was in her room. She learned that trick from a book about the Mossad that Dad bought us one Hanukkah.

I open the door and catch the string so I can put it back after.

To my surprise, she's redecorated since the last time I was in here. The Disney stuff is gone, replaced by gymnastic posters.

Sweet Caroline loves gymnastics. I keep hoping she'll break her neck on the parallel bars, but so far I've been unlucky on that front. Why can fate wipe out an entire village in Southeast Asia that's minding its own business, but my sister can do death-defying leaps on gymnastics equipment and stay healthy? It's not fair.

I stare at a giant photo of the Israeli rhythmic gym-nastics team in some kind of sexy human pyramid. Just what I need. More girls in tights. Between Sweet Caroline's meets and Mom's yoga classes, I'm having a tough adolescence.

It's kind of gross to get turned on in your sister's room, so I get down to business, looking through drawers, sliding open the closet, checking the shelves. There's nothing interesting, or at least nothing I can use against her. I think about where I would hide something that I didn't want anyone to find.

I check under her mattress. I search under the bed.

I look between her books.

I'm ready to give up my search when I see an Old Testament on the shelf. A birthday gift from Herschel last year. Just what every little girl wants. A Jewish Bible.

I open it, and a paper falls out. It's covered in sparkly stickers. I recognize Sweet Caroline's handwriting.

I start to read.

Bingo.

It's a love letter written to someone named Levi.

Every time she writes his name, she dots the *i* with a heart. Sickening.

Sweet Caroline + Levi. Levi + Sweet Caroline. Over and over again.

What is it with our family? We don't fall in love; we go insane.

I slip the letter into my pocket. I have leverage against her if I need it.

Sweet Caroline is in love. That seems impossible. She's only twelve years old. How would she know what love felt like, anyway?

"Excruciating."

That was the word Ms. Shine gave at the end of the spelling bee. It was down to Judi and me by that time, and since we kept spelling everything correctly, the words kept getting more difficult. Finally, we got to *excruciating*, which is a crazy word for second graders, but it shows you how smart we were. Or how smart we thought we were, because when Judi got the word, she smiled like she had it nailed, then proceeded to spell it wrong. She put in an *shi* instead of a *ci*.

Sucker.

Now it was my turn.

I had a lot of experience with *excruciating*. I'd studied it the night before.

All I had to do was get the word right, and I'd win.

I looked towards Judi. Her fists were clenched and there was sweat on her forehead. Her face was covered in freckles. There was even a freckle on her lip I hadn't seen before. Freakish.

It was obvious that she was nervous, but what did I care? I was going to crush her.

I started to spell the word, but I made the mistake of glancing at her again.

Something was different.

She had the same freckled face, but now she didn't seem so ugly to me. The idea of winning didn't feel fun anymore. It felt almost cruel.

I realized I wanted Judi to do well in the spelling bee. I still wanted to win, but not if it meant she had to lose.

So I blew the word. On purpose.

When it went back to Judi, she spelled it correctly. And she won.

"*Hah!* Got you!" she said, and she smiled at me.

I didn't care because for the first time in my life, losing made me happier than winning.

After that, Judi liked me. We became friends. We studied together. We competed with each other. We pushed each other to do better.

Sometimes I was number one and she was number two. Sometimes the order was reversed. But it didn't matter because we were the two smartest kids in class.

When Valentine's Day rolled around, Ms. Shine made us write cards to everyone in the class. We walked around and put them in baskets on the front of the desks.

When Judi passed by, she didn't put anything

in my basket. She whispered, "Check your cubby."

That's where I found her card later. The one where she asked me to be her boyfriend.

Judi and I did everything together after that. I dreamed about her. I smelled her when she wasn't there. I heard her voice in my head.

We were boyfriend and girlfriend for a week. The greatest week of my life.

They say God created the earth in seven days.

Six days. He rested on the seventh.

He created me in the same amount of time. And destroyed me.

Because after a week, something happened, and it was over. Judi wanted nothing to do with me anymore. She stopped talking to me. She walked by my desk without so much as looking at me.

And I never knew why.

One time I tried to ask her, and she burst into tears and ran away.

It was over. A week of bliss followed by years of longing.

Second grade. It was the Golden Age of Sanskrit.

I had a best friend, Herschel, who lived down the street.

I had a girlfriend, Judi Jacobs.

I had parents. Plural.

I had a kid sister, who was briefly adorable, innocent, and legitimately sweet.

Zadie Zuckerman was still alive, and I wasn't trapped in Jewish school.

I had it all. And then I lost it all.

I hadn't studied history yet, so I didn't know that all great eras end. Civilizations rise and fall. Cities prosper and decline.

Families come together and split apart.

Such is the cycle of life.

Second grade is when I learned not to trust good times. They seem like they're here forever, but they can come crashing down around you.

Sweet Caroline doesn't know this. She thinks she's in love. She thinks she's safe.

I know better.

"Mucous. Lots of it."

One of the ladies in Mom's prenatal yoga class is complaining about it. From the head nods around the room, it's obvious the other mommies-to-be know all about the mucous. I don't see any boxes of tissues around, so I get the feeling that whatever is stuffed up, it's not their noses.

"Mucous is very natural," Mom says. "It's the body's way of celebrating life."

"And phlegm is the throat's way of saying good morning," I say.

A few of the women chuckle. I like making women in tights laugh.

"My son is very funny," Mom says, "but these are serious matters."

She smiles but I can tell she's annoyed. She always smiles at me when we're at the Center and there are students watching.

"Rebekah, I think we're freaking out your son," an

Indian woman says. She has dark, exotic features and a massive bulge in her middle.

Mom walks a few steps towards me and wraps herself around my back.

"Is that true, Sanskrit? Are you freaking out?"

"Not at all. What's a little mucous between friends?" I say, and the women giggle.

Mom squeezes me even harder.

"All this will be yours in fifteen years," she announces to the ladies.

"I'm sixteen," I say.

"And I've been there for every moment of it," Mom says.

She laughs and smoothes down my hair. I don't see how it's funny that she doesn't know how old her son is.

"Alright, let's get started, ladies," Mom says. She presses a button on the sound system and the music of a Japanese flute fills the room. Mom hits a gong on a platform behind her. The sound swells, then drops away, the last bit of tone hanging in the air.

The women settle down on their mats. I told Mom I wasn't freaking out, but the truth is that I am, at least a little bit. Not because of mucous, but because I'm in a room full of women barely wearing clothes. In the winter the Center is a little easier to take because the women wear full leotards with tights or long flowing yoga skirts. But as summer approaches, the yoga clothes get smaller and smaller. Some women in the room today are wearing tights, others yoga pants, and some are wearing those stretchy shorts like volleyball players wear. They're like the bottom of a bathing suit, only there's no beach and no water. There's only me sitting ten feet away while they stretch with their legs wide open.

Let's just say I wear baggy shorts when I visit the Center. For my own protection and everyone else's.

"We'll begin on our backs in a relaxed pose."

The ladies lie back.

"My son is good at this one," Mom says, earning another laugh from the ladies.

I'm so glad I can be here to help Mom's comedy act.

I lie on my back. According to Mom this is called Dead Man's Pose, but she doesn't use that term today. I think it's bad luck to talk about death with so many babies-to-be in the room.

I look across at the sea of bumps. Some are little and some big, some wide and some narrow. I've seen pregnant women before, but never lying down with so few clothes on. When you see pregnant women out in the world they can look fat, but in tight yoga clothes you realize they're not fat at all. There's something growing inside them, and it's running out of room and wants to get out.

"Deep breath," Mom says. "Let your worries and cares drift away on the music. . . ."

I try to let my worries and cares drift, but they stick to me. First I worry about what's going on with school, then I worry about my deal with Sweet Caroline, then I worry about what Herschel said on the phone last night, about how I'm hurting people with my lie. Maybe even damaging my character.

Mom says, "Imagine there's an empty space inside of you and it's filling with warm, blue water. It is good. All is good."

All is not good, I think. Not for me, and not for these bumps, these babies-to-be. If they pop out into the world now, they're going to find themselves in yoga class, trapped in Dead Man's Pose with their obsessed mothers.

Because there's no escaping when you're a baby.

Wherever and whenever you're born, you start getting brainwashed. Maybe you have a grandfather who desperately wants you to practice Judaism, or a mother who forces you to do yoga, or a father who's spent ten years in a bedroom inventing something that still doesn't exist and probably never will. And these are the adults in your life who are supposed to be teaching you how to do things.

I look out across the bumps, and I feel bad for them. As soon as they pop out, the world is going to start pushing them in different directions, and what chance do they have?

"Now let the water flow out of you," Mom says.

"I'm waiting for my water to flow," one of the ladies says, followed by giggles.

I imagine crawling up to the first lady's stomach and telling the baby, "Don't come out. It's not safe. Pass it on."

That baby passes the message to the next, and on and on.

"Roll over on your sides, ladies. Let me know if you need help," Mom says.

But if I tell the babies not to come out, maybe there are going to be thirty stillbirths in the class, and they'll blame Mom. They'll say that all these women came to a prenatal class that killed their babies. Mom will have a terrible reputation, and it will ruin her life. If her life is ruined, my life is guaranteed to be ruined.

I decide I sent the wrong message. So I imagine going up to the first baby and saying, "Come out, but don't believe everything they tell you. Pass it on."

Then I think that might also be a bad message, because all these kids will be born not knowing who to trust. That's a terrible way to go through life, being surrounded by adults you can't trust.

That's when I decide I'm not the best person to be giving advice to fetuses.

"Mom," I whisper.

She shushes me.

"Bathroom."

She gives me a disappointed look.

"All this talk of water," I say, pulling at my shorts.

"Go ahead," she whispers.

I stand up. The ladies look at me.

"Mucous break," I say, and they giggle as I head for the door.

"Sat nam."

That's a mantra, a phrase you repeat over and over again in meditation. Mom told me it means something like, *Truth is my identity*. But truth is not exactly my strong point these days.

It's playing on a meditation CD piped into the bathroom.

Sat nam. Sat nam.

Anyway, *Sat nam* sounds more like, *Sit down*. Which is a pretty good mantra for the bathroom.

It's like the bathroom is inviting me to do my business.

So I open a stall and avail myself of the invitation.

The nice part about the men's room at the Center is that it's rarely used because there aren't many men to use it. There are guys who take yoga, but the female to male ratio is something like a hundred to one. While this is easy on the eyes, it's also easy on the men's room.

Privacy. When you share a bathroom with two women at home, you look for it wherever you can get it.

Sit down. The mantra beckons me.

I'm about to let rip when I hear the men's room door open.

I'm hoping this person is going to pee and get out of the bathroom fast so I can enjoy some quality time. But that's not what happens. I hear the sound of fabric moving, and then whoever it is joins the *sat nam* chorus with his own *sat nam*s.

I clear my throat a couple times to make my presence known, but the chanting doesn't stop. The guy actually starts to harmonize with the CD. The sound is beautiful and eerie, filling the bathroom with a spiritual chorus.

The stall next to me opens. Fabric rustles, and a man groans and sits down next to me.

Blue fabric spills under the wall of the stall, a robe or something that's coming into my stall. I try to discreetly shuffle the fabric away with my foot, but there's too much of it.

With another groan, the person lets go a fusillade, so loud and uncensored that I let out a little shout.

I kick the blue fabric over, and I stand up and fight to get my pants up.

There's another burst of body noise followed by more groans.

It's too much for me.

I flush my toilet fast and push out of my stall. I'm washing my hands when a voice says, "Excuse me."

I ignore it, turn the water up.

"Have you any tissue?" the voice says in lightly accented English.

I don't want to talk to a stranger in a men's room stall. I turn off the water and head for the bathroom door.

"Excuse me," the voice says more urgently.

"What?" I say. Now I'm annoyed.

"Tissue. To clean oneself."

"You mean toilet paper?"

"Please."

I look around for a roll of toilet paper, but there's nothing. Damn it.

I go into my stall and figure out how to remove the toilet paper from the holder. It's that scratchy recycled stuff that Mom buys for the Center and the house. You wipe yourself, and it feels like your butt survived the Six-Day War. I yank on it until I free the roll from the holder.

"I'll throw it over the top of the stall," I say.

"Don't throw it," the man says.

The stall door swings open.

A strange man with a giant beard sits on the toilet, fabric spilling around him in every direction. I scream and drop the toilet paper. I race out of the bathroom.

"Mom!" I shout as I run through the Center. I throw open the door to the yoga studio and it smashes against the wall with a loud bang.

The pregnant ladies scream.

"Mom!"

"What is it?"

"There's a strange man in the bathroom. He might be homeless. I think he broke in there or something."

"He may have wandered in," Mom says calmly. "The homeless are not bad people, Sanskrit. They're suffering. We've had this conversation."

"He opened the stall door, Mom. While he was on the toilet. That's not right."

I'm emphasizing words so she'll understand this is a crisis, not another opportunity to practice kindness and compassion with the less fortunate, particularly the less fortunate she's not related to, which is her forté.

"I'll take care of it," Mom says.

I'm a little surprised. This is a Mom I don't know, the strong and in-charge one who only appears at work.

"Don't go in there alone," one of the ladies says.

"We'll go with you, Rebekah," another one says.

A group of about ten of us edge our way down the hall. More ladies come out of the other yoga studio and join us.

"He was in here?" Mom says. She points towards the men's room.

"Right in there."

"How did he get past reception? Where's Crystal?"

"I don't know," I say.

"Do we need a weapon?" one of the women says. She's a young Asian woman, I think her name is Sally. She grabs a rolled-up yoga mat from the rack and grips it like a baseball bat. It seems an ineffective choice given the situation, but I'm thinking the homeless man can't overpower me and two dozen pregnant women. He's probably going to back down and run out of the place. But you never know.

"Maybe we should call the police, Mom."

"We don't need the police. We can take care of this. People are people, Sanskrit."

That's when I realize Mom isn't in charge; she's naïve. People are not people. People are dangerous. Not everyone takes deep breaths and eats organic. Some of them bring bombs onto buses in Jerusalem or stand you up at your parent-professor conference. Not that those two things are equal, but you know . . .

We approach the bathroom door with Mom leading us forward. She reaches out to open it, when it suddenly swings open on its own.

The ladies scream.

The homeless man steps out. He looks a little less homeless in the daylight. His hair is too long, his beard unkempt and scraggly. He's wrapped in bright blue fabric that hangs all the way to the floor.

He looks up, surprised at the army of pregnant women glaring at him.

"That's him," I say.

Mom gasps.

"Guru Bharat," she says. "You're here!"

"*Namaste.*"

That's what this guy says to my mother. *Namaste. The god in me recognizes the god in you.* He presses his hands together at chest level.

"*Namaste,*" Mom says, returning the greeting.

"My dearest Rebekah," the guru says.

I can hear his accent now. It's that light British accent you hear in people who go to British schools in foreign countries.

"I am most honored to be in your presence," he says. He bows from the waist and stays there, his head towards the ground.

"Guru!" Mom says, and she falls to her knees.

The ladies follow her lead. Women are dropping like flies all around me. The really pregnant ones have to struggle their way down. The less pregnant women just plop.

I'm the only one still standing. The guru comes out of his bow, and we're looking at each other face to face.

I feel a tug at my pant leg.

"Down," Mom whispers.

"No."

"Bow down."

"Jews don't bow down, Mom. We have a long history of not bowing down."

Mom is persistent. It's not like I can kick her, but I shuffle my leg around to try and get her hand off of me.

"Sanskrit, please!" Mom says, still tugging at me.

"Sanskrit?" the guru says.

Finally, somebody who can pronounce my name correctly.

"I've heard a lot about you," the guru says.

"You have? From who?"

"From your mother. We spoke on the computer. What do you call it?"

"Chatting?"

"Yes. We chatted. She's very proud of you."

"She is?" I say.

"Enough, ladies. Get up, please," the guru says.

The women rise as the guru walks over and stands in front of Mom.

"I can't believe you're here," she says.

"I'm here," he says, and smiles at her.

"May I—" she says, and holds out her arms.

"Please do," he says, and they embrace, a long, tight embrace, so intense that Mom all but disappears into his robes.

It goes on for way too long, to the point where the ladies and I are standing around, looking at one another uncomfortably.

"What the hell, Mom," I say.

She emerges from his robes, her face glowing.

"Thank you," she says to him.

"No, thank you. It's not often I get to hug a beautiful yogini."

I clear my throat loudly.

"I'm sorry I scared your son earlier," the guru says.

"You didn't scare me," I say.

"Why did you run from me?"

I want to tell him that we keep the stall door closed in America, especially when we look like crazy homeless men, but I glance at Mom and decide it would be better to keep that to myself.

Mom says, "We're all surprised that you're here, Guru Bharat. You honor us with your visit."

"No, no. It's my honor to be at your center," he says, like he's at the center of the world rather than the yoga center next to a waxing salon in Brentwood.

"May I show you around?" Mom says.

"That would be most gracious of you," the guru says.

"What about the prenatal class?" I say.

My being here for the class was important to Mom. Or so she said.

"The guru came all the way from India," Mom says. "I'm sure the ladies—"

"We don't mind," one of the pregnant ladies says.

"We don't," another one says. "Of course not."

I say, "I just think when you make a commitment, you should keep your commitment."

"What's that supposed to mean?" Mom says.

"I came here to help you. I could have been in school right now."

"Since when do you want to be in school?"

"Since I'd like to get into college, Mom. If that's okay with you."

"You're only a junior," Mom says. "You've got another year."

"It's Jewish school, Mom. We're worrying about college from day one."

"I'm sorry, guru," Mom says. "I don't think Sanskrit understands that we have the founder of a religious order in our midst."

"It's not a religious order," the guru says.

"What is it?" Mom says.

"It's nothing," the guru says.

He smiles and claps his hands, delighted with himself.

"How can it be nothing?" Sally says.

"The Buddha called it *sunyata*. Emptiness. There is no essential nature to things. We give them meaning, when they deserve none."

"That's upbeat," I say.

Mom throws me a look. "We want to learn all about it, guru," she says. "Just give me a minute to speak to my son."

Mom grabs me and pulls me into a yoga studio.

"Don't ruin this for me!"

That's what Mom says after she closes the door.

"Who the hell is this guy? Why haven't I heard anything about him?"

"First of all, this is my private life," Mom says. "I don't have to tell you everything I do."

"How private could it be? The whole yoga center knows."

"They don't know the details."

"What are the details? You have a creepy international boyfriend?"

"He's not my boyfr—you are so frustrating to me right now."

Mom stamps her foot on the ground. She's about to say something when she stops herself. Instead, she takes a yoga breath and closes her eyes.

"I'm not a kid," I say. "Why don't you just tell me the truth."

Mom exhales.

"The truth is this man is a very famous teacher from India who happens to be a new friend of mine. More than a friend. An inspiration."

"What's his name again?"

"Guru Bharat."

"Bharat?"

"It's a Hindu name for India."

"He named himself after a country? That's pretty arrogant."

Maybe I shouldn't be so critical because I'm named after a language. But that's Mom's fault, not mine. What if I changed my name to *United States*? U. S. Zuckerman. It sounds like a Jewish battleship.

"He didn't name himself," Mom says. "The name was bestowed on him. It's a great honor."

"How did you meet this person?"

"We met online after I saw his YouTube videos."

"YouTube is not a spiritual place, Mom. It's more like a place where cats play the piano."

"That's not true, honey. He has an amazing YouTube channel, and when I saw him, I knew he had a message for me. For my life. I wrote to him, and he wrote back. We've been e-mailing for a few months. Isn't that incredible? And now he's here!"

"What does he want?"

"You're being paranoid."

"I'm not paranoid. I'm appropriately cautious."

Dad taught me that people always want something

from you, even when they pretend they don't. *Especially* when they pretend they don't.

"If you must know, he's fascinated by American spirituality. I think he's come to see it for himself."

"Not to see you?"

Mom blushes.

"Now I understand," Mom says, and messes with my bangs. "You're being overprotective. It's sweet."

"I'm just saying you need to be careful. You don't really know this guy."

"What do you say we get to know him?" Mom says. "We can show him around the Center together."

"You go," I say. "I already met him in the bathroom. And I was less than impressed."

"Is that what a guru looks like?"

This is what I ask Crystal, the receptionist. I'm shy about talking to her because she wears halter tops that barely cover her chest and she's in a Ph.D. program at UCLA. Between her breasts and her brains I usually can't form English sentences around her. But she's the only one not chasing the guru around the Center right now.

"All gurus look different," she says, "but that is the one and only Guru Bharat."

"They don't have combs in India?"

"He's famous for his hair. It's been growing for more than a decade. Ever since he made his famous pronouncement."

"What pronouncement?"

"That nothing matters."

"And?"

"That's the whole pronouncement," she says.

"Nothing matters. That's his great spiritual contribution?"

"It's not as simple as that. He's taking Buddhist principles and updating them so we can understand."

"In other words, he's dumbing it down."

She crosses her arms, and the top shifts.

"You should go on YouTube and check it out. You're a spiritual guy. I think you'd be into it."

"I'm not a spiritual guy. I hate most religious stuff."

"So does he. You actually have a lot in common. You know how religious people are always preaching to us, telling us how we should act? Guru Bharat turned that on its head. He had the courage to tell the truth. Nothing that we do matters. Nothing changes anything. There is no way to be good."

"If nothing matters, what use is any of it?"

"Don't get angry with me; I didn't say it. It's the guru."

"How do you know all this?" I say.

"Your mom's been talking about him forever."

"How long is forever?"

"A few months at least. I can't believe he really came to Brentwood!"

The group comes walking around the corner, a buzz of nearly nude women around a tumble of sheets with a beard. Mom is saying, "If we knew you were coming, we could have welcomed you properly."

"This is welcome aplenty," the guru says.

Who says *aplenty*? It's ridiculous.

"We would have honored you with a feast," Mom says.

"We can take him to dinner," Sally says.

"We can go for Indian food!" one of the women says.

"Do you want to go for Indian food, Guru Bharat?" Sally says.

"To be honest, I'm rather tired of Indian food."

"Of course you are," Mom says. "We'll take you for vegetarian food, American-style. Let's go to A Votre Sante."

A Votre Sante. That's Mom's favorite restaurant. She took me there the last time we went to dinner together.

"I'm breaking a juice fast tonight," Mom says, "and I want it to be special."

The women head towards the changing room to get ready, and I edge over to Mom.

"You said that we were going to break your fast together," I say.

Mom looks towards the guru.

"I'll take you to dinner a different night," she says.

"You promised tonight."

She sighs, frustrated. I notice she's frustrated with me a lot lately.

"Why don't you come with us?" Mom says.

"That's not the same thing."

"I think you're being selfish," Mom says. "Why can't you help me? Why does everything have to be a fight?"

"It's not a fight—" I start to say, but I stop myself. Because if I disagree with Mom, then it is a fight. At least in her mind. Anything short of total agreement is a fight.

She doesn't want a son; she wants a follower. No wonder she likes the guru.

"Forget it," I say.

"No. Not forget it," Mom says. "I made you a promise, and I'd like to keep that promise at a later date if it's alright with you."

"It's not alright with me."

She glances over her shoulder at the guru.

"I don't understand you, Sanskrit. What if Jesus came to visit? Would you leave him to fend for himself at dinnertime?"

"We're Jews. We don't believe in Jesus."

"You're a Jew," she says. "Not me."

"Don't say that."

It's one thing to feel like you're not a Jew, but it's something else to say it out loud like that.

"If you don't want to hear the truth," Mom says, "that's your issue, not mine."

"Let's drop the subject," I say. "I'll get dinner with Sweet Caroline and do my homework."

Mom exhales, relieved. She puts her arm on my shoulder.

"I like when you kids do things together," she says.

"I know you do," I say.

Mom reaches into her pocket and comes out with a twenty. That's one of her best parenting tricks. Folded twenties. Unfortunately, they only arrive for necessities like food. We never get one to have fun or buy something crazy.

Unless Dad is around, that is. Then she likes to whip them out just to show Dad what a loser he is. Zadie wanted Dad to work for him in the terry business, but Dad refused and tried to start his own business, thereby dooming us to a life of poverty and handouts. That's how Mom tells the story, and she's never forgiven him for it.

Mom looks towards the guru now and makes a big point of handing over the money.

I'm a good mother, guru. Look at me taking care of my family.

I want to throw the money on the floor and stamp on it, but to be honest, I'm hungry and that would be counterproductive. I smile like I'm a good son and she's a good mother.

"Take care of your sister," she says. As if Sweet Caroline and I are close. Now who doesn't want to hear the truth?

"Thanks, Mom!" My voice is cheerful, too loud. I'm trapped in a movie I don't want to be a part of.

Mom tussles my hair, then walks back towards the guru.

"Have fun, you two!" I say, and I wave good-bye.

The guru is watching me, his face placid. I move, and his eyes follow.

I stare back at him, and he smiles.

It's a kind smile, but it reminds me a little of Barry Goldwasser. A smile for no reason, so you don't know if the person likes you or if they're making fun of you.

"I'm worried about you."

That's what Talya Stein's mother says when she sees me. I walk out of the Center, and she's right there on San Vicente getting into a Lexus. I'm so surprised, I almost run away.

"How is your mother?" she says.

"Touch and go."

"Oh my God," she says.

I gesture back towards the Center. "I was just taking care of a few things for her."

What if Mom walks out of the Center right now? I have to get rid of Mrs. Stein fast.

"We're all with you," she says. "You know that."

I know that her daughter, Talya Stein, wears tight, long-sleeved sweaters and has barely spoken to me in three years. I know she's best friends with The Initials. That's all I know.

"I have to go," I say.

"Of course. Shabbat is starting soon," she says. "Do you have dinner plans, Aaron?"

I think about sitting at a dinner table with Talya Stein. Maybe we'd hit it off, and that would connect me back to The Initials. But probably not. She'd probably hate me for being in her house, only she'd pretend to like me because I'm going through a family tragedy. I can't take something like that tonight.

"I'm going to the hospital with my sister," I tell Mrs. Stein.

"If you change your mind," she says.

I thank her and walk away fast.

I glance over my shoulder and I'm relieved to see her driving away.

I'm safe for now, but the clock is ticking on this lie. Somebody is going to see Mom, and I'll have serious explaining to do.

Maybe they'll even see her at A Votre Sante tonight, and the whole story will blow up. That might be a relief.

I hurry down San Vicente to Barrington, then I turn south and cross over Wilshire where Brentwood becomes West L.A., and the expensive houses become little houses and so-so apartments. West L.A. is on the doorstep to Brentwood, but it's a whole other world. A cheaper world. The real world. Or at least our version of it.

It's Friday night, a few minutes before sundown. All over the city, observant Jews are rushing home before Shabbat starts. Jewish mothers are putting pots on the stove in timed pressure cookers, setting the table for a big family dinner. Kids are taking showers and changing. Final calls are being made and important messages returned. From sunset to sunset, there will be no work done, no power used. There will be services and prayer and community. People remembering and honoring God.

At the same time all over the city, non-observant Jews are not observing, not setting timers or preparing, not even remembering Shabbat until they see the black hats walking to shul in their neighborhoods. What do they think then?

Do they feel guilty that they're not observant like their brothers and sisters?

Do they feel embarrassed that they belong to a religion where some people wear furry hats and long black coats and walk through the streets on Friday night and Saturday morning?

All religions have extremists, people who have drifted from the center towards the edges, others who have drifted from the edges back to the center. And still others like us who have drifted so far away that they don't remember who they are anymore.

Maybe that's what Zadie Zuckerman was worried about. Once he was no longer around, who would be there to urge us towards Judaism? Only his money is left to keep the fires lit at the Temple.

But how long will that last?

"Mom is in love."

I say it gravely, so Sweet Caroline will understand how serious the situation is.

"What does that have to do with our dinner?" Sweet Caroline says.

"We're not getting any dinner. We have an absentee mother. I'm trying to explain the situation to you."

"She gave you a twenty, didn't she?" Sweet Caroline says.

She knows how Mom works. Instead of taking care of us, she gives us the means to take care of ourselves. It's like the United Nations food program.

"We can go to Whole Foods," Sweet Caroline says.

"With twenty dollars? So much for dessert. Besides, if we go to Whole Foods, we'll run into people from the neighborhood, which means we'll run into people from school, which means we'll have to do a lot of lying about Mom. So let's just make something here."

"Fine," Sweet Caroline says. She snatches the twenty out of my hands. "I'll take it as payment. You're good for this week. But Monday is coming up fast."

"Mom is in love, and you're worried about blackmailing me."

"Mom's always in love," she says.

Sweet Caroline has a point.

Mom falls in love with things all the time. She fell in love with hot yoga, then elastic band yoga, then, briefly, nude yoga. Nude yoga was rough on me. I couldn't use the bathroom in our house for three months. Mom would be in there nude and sweaty, the hot water running on full, steam pouring out the crack at the bottom of the door. By the time that trend passed, the floorboards outside the bathroom door were warped.

Mom fell in love with poetry for five minutes when she took a class at UCLA. The house was filled with notebooks, scraps of paper, even parchment when she thought writing on parchment with a feather would make her more creative.

She fell in love with a particular juice at a local health food store. But it was too expensive, so she started juicing at home. For six months, I was woken up at 4:30 every morning by the growl of a juicing machine engine revving in our kitchen. We all had to drink it, to the point where our toilet bowl turned green from all the chlorophyll.

Mom falls in love with many things, all of them briefly but intensely.

Maybe that's what love is. You lose yourself. You go insane. But it's temporary insanity.

So why does this time feel different to me?

"Did Mom tell you she's in love?" Sweet Caroline says.

"No. But I can tell."

"Who's the guy?"

"He's weird."

"The last one was weird. They're all weird."

The last one was a middle-aged, out-of-work actor who served juice samples at Erewhon, the natural food market near The Grove. I blame him for bringing wheat grass into our lives.

"This one is an Indian guru," I say.

"That's a racist thing to say."

Sweet Caroline's class did a unit on racism last month, and now she sees it everywhere she looks.

"I'm not racist," I say.

"If you hate Indians, you're racist."

"I don't hate Indians. I hate gurus."

"Then you're prejudiced."

I think about that for a second. Do I hate the guru because he's a guru? Because he hasn't cut his hair in ten years? Or do I hate him because Mom likes him?

"He came all the way from India to visit Mom," I say.

"That is weird," Sweet Caroline says, thinking it over.

"That's what I'm trying to tell you. I've got a bad feeling."

"You worry too much," Sweet Caroline says.

"You don't worry enough."

"I'll tell you what's going to happen. Mom will be a freak for a couple weeks, then she'll go back to being our mom."

The doorbell rings.

I look through the peephole. It's a man with a giant gift basket. I open the door and take it from him.

I look at the card.

GET WELL SOON,
FROM YOUR FRIENDS
AT THE BRENTWOOD JEWISH ACADEMY

I bring it into the kitchen.

"What's that?" Sweet Caroline says.

"Our dinner is here," I say.

I put the basket down and pull off the plastic wrap. The basket is overflowing with fruit and chocolate. I take the card and rip it into little pieces so it's unreadable. Then I start to separate out the chocolate.

"Is this because of Mom's accident?" Sweet Caroline says.

"Yes. And it won't be the last time we get one. We need a plan."

"You need a plan. I don't need anything."

"You're not getting twenty dollars a week to watch me do all the work."

"Okay, we can pretend I have a rich boyfriend."

I think of the love letter I found in Sweet Caroline's room. Levi. I want to ask her who he is, but I don't.

"You're too young to have a boyfriend," I say.

"I am not," she says. "Anyway, Mom is different about dating. She's not like those other mothers."

"Which mothers?"

"The ones who care about things like that."

"I care," I say, because the idea of my kid sister dating at twelve seems wrong. "I don't think you should be dating."

"You're not my parent," she says.

"I know that."

"So stop trying."

"My pleasure," I say.

She says, "If we say I have a boyfriend, it explains the gift baskets coming in."

I think about that for a second.

"Admit it. It's a good idea," she says.

"It's okay."

It's actually a brilliant idea, but I won't give her the satisfaction of telling her.

Sweet Caroline picks through the basket, sniffing at

a few things. She settles on a mini-bar of Toblerone. She takes it into her bedroom, even though we're not allowed to have food in our rooms.

I look through the basket, coming up with an expensive chocolate-and-caramel thing. I bite into it, and it's so good I have to sit down. I've spent my childhood eating Mom's equivalent of candy—chunky globs of carob sweetened with fruit juice. Compared to that, a real piece of candy is like heaven.

I think about Mom eating dinner at A Votre Sante right now.

Maybe Sweet Caroline is right, and I'm worried about Mom and the guru for nothing.

But something in my gut tells me that this is different, and I should be worried. Even more worried than I already am.

I decide I'll talk to Mom about it when she gets back from dinner. More than just talk. I'll sit her down and ask her point-blank what's going on.

I go to my room and wait for her. I study for a while so I don't fall behind from missing school.

Eight o'clock becomes nine, nine becomes ten.

Mom doesn't get back.

I finally get into bed after eleven.

I can't sleep. I toss and turn, thinking about Mom at dinner for all these hours. She doesn't eat enough to spend four hours at a restaurant. So what is she doing for so long?

I think about God. In the Old Testament if you were having a crisis, you could pray to him and he might show himself.

Other times he would pop up completely unexpectedly, appearing in front of people to tell them what to do. Sometimes he told them they were in trouble, struck them down, or messed with their life in some way. That's not a God you want to have around on a regular basis, but at least you knew where you stood with him.

Now he never shows up. He doesn't appear, he doesn't speak, he doesn't punish or reward.

He does nothing. We're supposed to believe in him, have faith that he exists when there's no evidence at all.

I drift off to sleep wishing God would just show up and tell me what to do.

"He's come for you."

That's what the voice says, followed by loud knocking on my door.

I sit up fast in bed, waking from a deep sleep.

"Sanskrit. Wake up. He's here." Mom's voice.

The sun is shining through my blinds. It's morning.

"Who's here?" I say.

"It's your friend from down the street," Mom says. "The one who got really Jewish."

"Herschel? What's he doing here?"

I stumble out of bed, throw on some sweats.

I crack the door, but Mom is gone. I walk into the living room.

Herschel is standing there in a full suit, the white *tzitzit* threads hanging out, a black fedora on his head.

"I could get you some juice," Mom is saying to him.

"No, thank you," Herschel says.

Mom is setting the table, pulling items from a Whole

Foods bag and setting them out on plates like real mothers do in the morning. Or so I've heard.

Mom never sets the table, and we never get breakfast at home. Mom usually fasts in the morning or has a glass of juice. I can drink my breakfast or get something on the way to school. If I want to chew in the morning, I have to smuggle solid food into my room the night before. Pop-Tarts, bagels, muffins. It's like the Underground Railroad for breakfast pastries.

"Would you like a mango?" Mom asks Herschel.

He's looking at the gift basket on the counter.

"I'd offer you something from the basket, but—" She looks around, confused. "Sanskrit, what's this basket doing here?"

"A kid at Sweet Caroline's school. He's in love with her."

"That's so sweet," Mom says without so much as a blink, "but you know I don't allow sugar in the house."

"I guess her boyfriend didn't know that."

"We'll talk about this later." Mom frowns at the basket and spoons something green into a bowl. "Herschel, I bought some nice seaweed salad."

"I can't. Really."

"Why not?"

I say, "I hate to burst your bubble, Mom, but your food isn't kosher."

"Seaweed is kosher, isn't it? There's no meat in it."

"*We're* not kosher," I say. "Our kitchen isn't kosher."

"Oh, I'm sorry," she says, and goes back to whatever she's doing with the Whole Foods bags.

"What are you doing here?" I say to Herschel.

"I thought you might like to come with me."

"Where?"

"To shul."

"Shul? That's a terrible idea."

"But it's Shabbat," he says, like that's going to motivate me. "We could go to the synagogue at school if that would make you more comfortable."

"The whole idea makes me uncomfortable."

I try to remember the last time I went to a Shabbat service voluntarily.

Sweet Caroline walks in, still in her pajamas.

She looks from the food on the table, to Herschel, to me.

"Who died?" she says.

"Nobody."

"Why is there food in our house?"

"Mom is making breakfast."

"Is she on a new antidepressant?"

"Jesus. Give us a second, would you?" I say.

"Lord's name!" she says. She shakes a warning finger at me, then stamps off.

Herschel says, "Sorry to intrude. It's early."

"You're inviting me to services? That's why you came over?"

"I didn't plan it," Herschel says. "I was walking, and something led me here."

"Kind of you to offer," I say, "but—"

"Don't *but*. Just come with."

"I can't," I say.

"Can't or won't?"

"Can't," I say.

"Why not?"

I glance at the fruit-and-chocolate gift basket on the kitchen counter.

"You didn't take care of the thing at school," Herschel says.

"Shhh," I say, lowering my voice. "I will. First thing next week."

"Don't wait until next week. You've got everyone worried."

"There's nothing to worry about."

"They don't know that. You're causing them *tsuris*."

Tsuris. Yiddish for *pain*.

"Come to shul with me, Sanskrit. I think you want to."

"If you think that, then you don't know me as well as you used to," I say.

"Maybe not."

"You *want* to go to services, Herschel. You like it. I wish I could believe like you do."

"I don't just believe," Herschel says. "I question. I wonder. Just like you."

"Maybe so. But when you're done with all that questioning, where are you?"

"I'm with God."

"That's the difference between us. When I'm done . . ."

I look out into the living room at Mom's yoga mat, her Tibetan singing bowl, the little altar she's set up in the corner for meditation.

"Where are you when you're done?" Herschel says.

"I'm alone."

He rolls a *tzitzi* thread between his fingers.

"I didn't come to beg," he says. "Only to extend the offer."

"I pass."

He shrugs and heads for the door.

"If you change your mind . . . ," he says, and then he's gone.

Mom putters in and goes back to setting the table. The timing is a little too perfect. Was she listening at the door?

"It's nice to see Herschel," she says, "even if he doesn't look like Herschel anymore."

"He looks like Super Jew."

"That's not nice. He's a boy on a spiritual journey."

"That's not what I'd call it."

"Because you're jealous."

"Why would I be jealous? I just want my old friend back."

"I see," Mom says.

"You don't see."

"Maybe I don't."

I hate when Mom won't fight with me. She goes into this mode where she refuses to argue. She calls it her surrender mode, her Dead Bug pose. That's an actual pose in yoga where you lie on your back and put your hands and feet in the air like a suffocated cockroach. But she only does it when she doesn't want to deal with something. Usually me.

"What time did you get home last night?" I say.

"That's a rude question."

"When I go to sleep and my mother isn't home yet, it raises a few questions. That's fair, isn't it? To ask the question?"

"You're worse than your father."

"Maybe if you two communicated better, he wouldn't have left."

"Don't you—" Mom shakes with anger. She points her finger at me. "Don't you talk to your mother like that."

"Fine," I say.

"This is why I don't usually make breakfast," Mom says. "Because you don't appreciate me."

"Seaweed salad and mangoes isn't breakfast, Mom. It's what people eat after a shipwreck."

"For your information, there are also whole wheat bagels and Tofutti spread."

"Why are you making breakfast anyway?"

Sweet Caroline comes in. She's changed into sweats and a pink hoodie.

She takes one look at the seaweed salad and says, "I'm not hungry."

"Did this whole family wake up on the wrong side of the bed?" Mom says.

That's when the toilet flushes down the hall. A door opens and shuts followed by footsteps.

"What the hell?" I say, and I jump up.

The guru walks into our living room. Today, he's wrapped in bright orange robes and a turban.

"Mom!" Sweet Caroline screams, jumping behind her for protection.

"*Sat nam*, Zuckerman family," the guru says. He looks at our surprised expressions. "Was I not expected?"

"I was trying to tell them," Mom says.

"Who the hell is that?" Sweet Caroline says.

"This is my guru," Mom says. "He's come all the way from India to spend time with us."

My guru? When did he become her personal guru?

Mom smiles and opens her arms wide, like she's presenting us with a gift.

Sweet Caroline looks at me, concerned. I nod. *This is the one I was telling you about.*

"Guru, you remember Sanskrit," Mom says.

"I seem to have a habit of shocking him," the guru says with a smile.

"You keep showing up where you're not wanted," I say. "That's pretty shocking."

"Sanskrit!" Mom says.

"No, no. He has a point," the guru says. "It's not easy to open your heart to a stranger."

"It's not my heart. It's my bathrooms that are off limits."

I'd like to see the guru lose his temper, but I'm not sure he has one. No matter what I say he grins and looks calm. I was right. He's definitely got Barry Goldwasser syndrome.

"Who is this lovely creature?" the guru says, referring to my sister.

"This is my youngest, Sweet Caroline," Mom says.

"An apt name. I can feel the sweetness in your aura, little one," the guru says.

Obviously, his powers of perception leave something to be desired.

Sweet Caroline smiles. I hope she's not falling for it, but she's been known to succumb to compliments, especially from men.

"What's he doing in our house?" I say.

"He needed someplace to stay," Mom says.

"Where did he sleep?" I say.

"Sanskrit. That's rude," Mom says.

"I understand why you would be concerned," the guru says. "I slept right here."

He points to the meditation area in our living

room. He smiles at me. Which only makes me hate him more.

"He's a visitor," Mom says. "What does your religion say about visitors, Sanskrit?"

"You mean *our* religion," I say.

"My point is he's come a long way," Mom says, "and it's our responsibility to offer him hospitality."

"That's why they have hotels," I say.

"He's a guru," Mom says.

"Gurus like hotels. When the Dalai Lama comes, he stays at a suite in the Ritz Carlton," I say.

"No, he doesn't," Mom says.

"It's true," Sweet Caroline says. "I read it in the *L.A. Times.*"

"See that?" I say.

"I don't think that's the truth," Mom says.

"Actually, his Holiness stays at the Montage," the guru says. "He has a lot more money than I have."

"I thought Buddhists took a vow of poverty," I say.

"Individually, yes. But his organization raises money to spread the word of the dharma."

I think about Rabbi Silberstein pushing High Holy Days tickets. Maybe Tibet and Brentwood aren't so different.

"Why doesn't *your* organization have money?" I say.

"We have nothing to spread. If people want what we have, they will find us. That's what we believe. Therefore, money is not needed."

"You can't live without money," I say. "Everyone knows that."

"Dad lives without money," Sweet Caroline says.

"Zadie had money," I say. "You barely remember because you were so young."

"I remember," she says.

"I do not want to talk about your zadie," Mom says. "Not when we have such interesting *living* people in the room." She sits down at the table. "Let's have breakfast and get to know each other."

The three of us look at her.

"You can't just push a guru on us at breakfast," I say. "Right, Sweet Caroline?"

She sits down.

Traitor.

The guru and I stay standing, looking at each other.

"May I join you, Sanskrit?" the guru asks.

I can see what he's doing. Trying to give me space, trying to win me over by being deferential. I'm not falling for it.

"You can eat, but then you have to go," I say.

"Sanskrit!" Mom says.

"What? We don't have enough space as it is. Much less enough food."

Mom tenses like she's about to get into it with me, then, just as quickly, she lets the anger drain from her. She makes one of those motions like she's pulling an invisible string from her chest. She takes a deep breath, and her voice softens.

"It's strange to have a new person here. I understand."

"You don't understand," I say.

The guru and I are still standing, looking at each other.

"Can we just have breakfast like civilized people?" Mom says.

"Since when are we civilized?" I say.

I look to Sweet Caroline for support. I don't get any.

"Please have breakfast with us," Mom says. "I got you some organic breakfast bars. I know you like those."

I look at the guru, all wrapped up in flowing orange robes. The man who believes in nothing, yet has followers wherever he goes.

He's not going to add me to his list.

"I changed my mind," I say. "I'm not hungry."

I grab my backpack and storm out of the house.

"They will find us."

That's what the guru said earlier. The people who want what he has will find him. Is that what happened with Mom? She was looking for something, anything, and this is what she found?

The thought makes me sick inside. The idea that my mother is one of those people who jumps at any trend, believing she's found the answer to life's questions.

That gets me thinking about Herschel.

He's at shul right now, sitting with everyone and praying. I consider going there to join him. I remember what that used to be like, the sound of voices in unison, calling out to God. The feeling of sitting in a group of believers. We would go as a family some- times, drive to Zadie's house, park the car, then walk from his place because he wouldn't use the car on Shabbat. We'd show up at Zadie's synagogue and everyone would greet him, pinch my cheeks, say how happy they were to see us and make space for us to sit down. Sometimes I'd even feel happy to be there.

I could go to shul with Herschel now, but it wouldn't be the same. I'd just be taking up space because I don't believe.

So I walk.

It's a warm Saturday in April, and I walk down San Vicente west towards Santa Monica. The exercisers are out en masse. There are runners, bikers, speed walkers, uniformed teams of cyclists. It seems like when you turn forty in Brentwood you have to join a cycling team, put on one of those skin-tight colored uniforms, and wear funny shoes that click when you walk into the coffee shop.

I move in the same direction as the exercisers, west, towards the ocean. I read somewhere that there is a high rate of suicide in California because people who are trying to escape their lives head west, and when they get here and find that nothing has changed, that they've run out of choices, they jump into the ocean or drive off Pacific Coast Highway.

It's an interesting theory, but what happens if your life starts here?

Where do you go?

"On your right!" a cyclist shouts, and goes flying by me, so close that I feel the wind blow the hairs on my arm.

"Watch it!" another one says.

I've wandered too close to the bike lane, and a riding team is shouting at me, territorial, ready to mow me down.

I jump to get out of one's way, and I end up in front of another. I dodge that one and the next one comes. One cyclist after another shouts rude things at me. It's like a hyena attack on one of those nature shows where they surround some defenseless animal and hound it until it collapses.

I'm that animal.

It seems to go on forever, the shouts and the wind and the rushing bikes. Finally, I can't take it anymore. I gather my courage, let out a roar, and spin around to face the pack.

But they're gone.

There are no bikes. They've all passed me by.

I'm alone on the median on San Vicente, ready to fight something that's not there.

"You're off balance, Sanskrit."

That's what Mom says when I walk back into the house an hour later.

"I'm not off balance," I say. I look around. The guru is gone. His stuff is out of the living room. "In fact, I'm feeling very balanced right now."

"What do you call your little outburst this morning?" Mom says.

"I'd say that was an appropriate reaction upon finding a strange man in your kitchen."

"Not so strange. You'd met him before."

"Not in my kitchen."

"First of all, it's not *your* kitchen. You don't pay the bills in this family."

A dead man pays the bills in this family. At least the tuition bills. But I don't say that to Mom.

"Forget it," Mom says. "I'm not having this fight again."

Mom unfurls a yoga mat and lies on it on the living room floor.

Her answer to everything. Kundalini.

"Join me," she says.

"I'm not in the mood."

"Please, Sanskrit."

"It's not a matter of *please*, Mom. I just don't feel like it."

"Why not?"

"I had a big breakfast. I don't want to be upside down right now."

"Where did you eat?"

"At Starbucks. I had a breakfast sandwich with extra bacon."

Mom makes a face. I call it her meat wince. She pretends she doesn't care that I eat meat, that it's my own personal choice and her only job is to inform me so I can make a good decision. But if I dare to walk in the house with an In-N-Out Burger bag, she can't control her reaction. It's like a beefy form of Tourette's.

"You can't do one little posture with me?" Mom says.

"I cannot. I am incapable of it."

Mom pushes up into a headstand. Now we're looking at each other eye to ankle. It's like a docking maneuver on the space shuttle. I imagine Mom and me lost in space together. I wonder what it would be like to be alone with Mom, nobody to interrupt us.

"Are you on drugs?" Mom says out of the blue.

"Are you kidding?"

"You're not addicted to bath salts?"

"What are bath salts?"

"My yoga blog talked about it in their Parent Corner. All the kids are doing it now."

"I'm not doing it."

"Well, everyone else is."

"Something else I can feel bad about. I'm not on drugs, Mom. They're not even popular in our school. Kids are more worried about Israeli politics than getting high."

Mom examines me upside down, trying to determine if I'm lying. "I made an appointment for you with Dr. Prem," she says.

Dr. Prem is not really a doctor. He's Mom's chiropractor.

"No!" I say, even though I like Dr. Prem. He's just weird like everyone else Mom knows.

"I'm trying to help you."

"How does getting my back cracked help me?"

Mom pinches her fingers together and gestures from her toes to her head.

"Flow," she says.

"I don't want to flow."

"It's already done. Two o'clock today. Your father is going to take you."

"Why aren't you taking me?" I say.

"I'm giving the guru a tour of the city," Mom says.

"Like you gave him a tour of your bedroom?"

Mom opens her mouth to respond, then takes a calming breath instead.

"You don't think I'm doing a good job as a parent?" she says.

I feel a drop of sweat pooling on my forehead. It hangs there for a moment before rolling down the side of my face.

"I didn't say that."

"But you've brought it up," Mom says. "A few times now."

I wipe my forehead with my sleeve.

"Don't wipe your head like that," Mom says. "It stains the fabric."

"Sorry."

"You don't appreciate what I do for you. I bought you that shirt."

"I know you did."

"Dr. Prem is expensive. So is your sister's doctor."

"I know."

"I'm trying to keep this family's head above water. I'm killing myself to build up the Center. I'm working all the time. You think I like being away from my children so much?"

"No," I say, even though I think the answer is yes.

"I even invited you to teach a class with me."

I stare at the floor.

"I'm doing my best, and you have the nerve to stand here and criticize me when I'm trying to help you. And maybe have a life of my own at the same time."

"Sorry," I say.

Mom drops out of her headstand and her feet whack the floor hard.

"Now you've got me disturbed, Sanskrit. I have to find my center again."

Mom breathes deeply, stretches, breathes again. She rubs her forehead, upset. I hate it when she's upset.

"I'll go to Dr. Prem and get adjusted," I say.

"You will?" Mom says.

"Anything you want."

"Anything?"

"Of course."

"Give me a kiss," Mom says.

"Gross."

"Not gross. I'm your mother."

She takes my head in her hands and plants a big, wet kiss on my cheek.

"My son," she says. "I'm feeling better now."

"I'm glad," I say.

Mom always feels better when she gets her way. And honestly, it's easier for everybody involved.

"Busy. Always very busy."

That's what Dad says when I climb into the car later
and ask him how he's doing. I have to clear a foot of
junk off the passenger seat before I can even sit down.

"Busy with what?" I say.

"I could tell you," he says. "But then I'd have to kill
you."

He chuckles like this is funny.

It's not. Child Protective Services would not take
kindly to jokes like this. It's not like I would call them,
but we're on their radar after Sweet Caroline got sick
of Mom's tempeh stew a few years ago and told her
teacher Mom was serving us dog food. The teacher
took her seriously and called the hotline, and when
the social workers showed up one night during dinner,
they took a look at our plates and thought she might be
telling the truth. Mom's tempeh stew was brought to a
lab for testing, and we spent the night at juvenile hall
eating bologna sandwiches and spicy Fritos.

The next day the test came back negative for meat products. Sweet Caroline got in big trouble for lying and we were returned to the house. Mom spent the next six months on a mission to prove how delicious vegetarian food can be.

As far as I'm concerned, the mission failed.

"What has you so busy?" I ask Dad. "In general terms."

"Dad's working on important things," Sweet Caroline says as she climbs into the back of the car. "Daddy, it's disgusting back here."

"I didn't get a chance to straighten up."

"That's okay," Sweet Caroline says as she pushes stacks of books and papers out of the way to make a space.

The car door doesn't close correctly in back, so she has to slam it, then pull it hard three times until it clicks.

"You're inventing things for the government, right, Daddy?"

"I can neither confirm nor deny," Dad says. "I only know I had to interrupt important work to be with you here today. To escort you on this critical mission, Sweet McGeet."

Dad has, like, fourteen pet names for Sweet Caroline. He only has two names for me. *Sanskrit* most of the time, and *Aaron* when he's angry at Mom and doesn't want to say the name she chose for me.

"Remind me. What is this important mission?" Dad says.

"See's Candies, Daddy," Sweet Caroline says.

"I *sees* a chocolate truffle in your future," Dad says with a smile.

I've heard that stupid joke fifty thousand times, but Sweet Caroline laughs like it's brilliant. She loves See's Candies. I wish the stuff would make her pudgy. It's hard to be arrogant when you're pudgy.

"Sound like we have a road trip on our hands!" Dad says, getting excited. "We had some crazy road trips in college. Back in the day, boy, the gearheads and I knew how to do it right."

Gearheads. That's what they called the engineers at Cal Tech when Dad went to school there.

"I have to go to Dr. Prem," I say. "That's why you're here, remember?"

"Oh, right," Dad says, depressed by the sudden appearance of responsibility. "And you have to be there at—"

He looks at the clock. It's 1:30.

"We're late!" he says.

"We have to be there by two," I say.

"But your mother said—"

"She gave you the wrong time because you're always late."

"Your mother is a real case, let me tell you."

"The psychologist said you're not supposed to say

bad things about Mom," Sweet Caroline says. "Even if you hate her."

"I don't hate her," Dad says.

"Resent her then," Sweet Caroline says.

"Where did you learn a word like that?"

"From the psychologist, Daddy. Plus, I read. Unlike some people."

She kicks the back of my seat, but I ignore her.

Dad throws the car in reverse and shoots out of the driveway, narrowly missing an oncoming SUV.

"Watch out!" I say.

"That guy can watch out," Dad says. "I'm trying to back out of my own driveway."

It's not Dad's driveway anymore, but I don't need to remind him of that. Instead I say, "That's not how it works, Dad. The oncoming driver has the right of way."

"In what universe?" Dad says.

"In our universe," I say.

"I don't like our universe," Dad says. "That's why I'm inventing a new one."

"Can I be in your universe, Daddy?" Sweet Caroline says.

"You are the queen of the new universe," Dad says.

"If anyone smells throw up, it's mine," I say.

"That's disgusting," Sweet Caroline says.

"Where is Attack of the Mummy's office again?" Dad says.

Dr. Prem is a Sikh, so he wears all white. Dad calls him Attack of the Mummy.

"In Beverly Hills. Remember?" I say.

"Oh, that's right," Dad says. "Poop bird."

He presses the brakes too hard and pulls an illegal U-turn in the middle of Wilshire Boulevard. A bunch of plastic water bottles slide by my feet.

"Why do you need so much water?" I ask Dad.

"What if the big one happens while we're driving?"

The big one. The great Los Angeles earthquake.

Dad taps his head. "Water. It's the key to life."

"Better safe than sorry," I say.

"That's right," Dad says, like he's taught me a valuable lesson.

"Daddy, have you gotten any calls from school?" Sweet Caroline says.

I throw a warning glance towards the backseat.

"Why would I get a call from your school?"

"From *Sanskrit's* school." Sweet Caroline corrects him.

"No calls," he says. "At least I don't think so. I'm not big on listening to messages. Is there a problem?"

"No problem," I say.

Dad sounds leery. He's not good with problems.

Sweet Caroline says, "They're doing some fund-raising for next year."

"Fund-raising? Oh, no," Dad says.

Sweet Caroline smiles back at me, and suddenly I go

from hating her to thinking she's a genius. Dad doesn't have much money, and if he thinks the school is calling to ask for some, he will avoid them at all costs.

In other words, we're safe.

For now.

"Nice to see you again, Zuckerman family."

This is how Dr. Prem's office manager greets us when we walk in. What family is she talking about? Calling us a family is like calling an asteroid a planet. It's not a planet. It's part of a planet. The shattered remains of a planet, thrust out of its orbit and shooting through space.

She doesn't care. She's just happy to see us.

"Zuckerman family, reporting for quackery," Dad says, and he salutes.

"Cut it out, Dad," I say.

It takes guts to walk into a doctor's office and call them quacks. It's sort of stupid, too. You don't want to piss off your doctor before he works on you. Especially a chiropractor. What if instead of an adjustment, he decides to snap your neck like James Bond? If anyone knows how to do that, it's a chiropractor.

"I'm sorry," Dad says. " I thought you hated it here."

"I don't hate it," I say, even though I do. "And keep your voice down."

I glance at the office manager.

"Whatever," Dad says. "We're here. And on time."

"Gold star for you!" the office manager says.

"Hey, this is my kind of place," Dad says.

Dad expects praise for doing things you're supposed to do, like showing up for your kid's appointment on time.

The office manager hands me my chart and directs me back to one of the carrels.

"Do you need me to come with you?" Dad says.

"It's not the dentist, Daddy," Sweet Caroline says. She's making herself tea from the dispenser.

When we were kids, Dad used to come into the dentist's with us because we were so afraid. He hated it even worse than we did. He said the sound of the drill reminded him of the machines at Zadie's terry cloth factory and gave him a migraine.

"I'll be fine," I say.

"Good luck then," Dad says, and he puts his arms straight out in front of him and moans like a mummy.

I head to the back, slip off my shoes, and lie down on the hard table. You're supposed to meditate while you wait for your adjustment. I listen to the sound of water from an electric fountain and a recording of someone chanting in a foreign language. I wonder if it's Sanskrit. The sad thing is, I wouldn't even know if it was because I don't speak any Sanskrit.

I arrange my neck pillow behind me, and I try to count my breaths. It doesn't work, so I try to focus on an object, a particular ceiling tile with a pattern that almost looks like a smiley face. When that doesn't work, I try to feel where my body is in space, monitoring my five senses. All of these are tricks I've learned from Mom. But instead of relaxing me, meditating just makes me think faster and faster. Why would anyone meditate if it just makes things louder?

I feel a gentle touch on my foot.

I look up into the smiling face of Dr. Prem and his white turban. I have nothing against Sikhs or people who wear white as a lifestyle choice, but I just don't believe in it. I don't believe in the power of white, or the healing magic of the Kundalini yoga he always talks about, or even alternative treatments like chiropractic. I come because it makes Mom happy. And it sort of feels nice when your back cracks.

"How are you, Sanskrit?" he says.

"I don't know."

"Let's find out," he says, and he starts to press different points on my body.

He presses the center of my chest, holds his hand there for a moment. I start to feel afraid. What if he can feel what's going on with me? The anger inside of me, the secrets I'm keeping. What if he could get all of it just by touching me, and the secrets came rushing out of my body without my being able to stop them?

He presses my chest again, but nothing bad happens. He simply says, "Very interesting."

I open my eyes. He's smiling at me.

"I don't believe in this," I say.

"Why do you come?"

"Because my mother wants me to."

"I like that," he says.

"You like that I don't believe in what you do?"

"No, I like that you were honest."

He leans towards me, his voice dropping to a whisper:

"We don't have to do the adjustment. I'll tell your mother I did it, but I won't charge her."

"That's okay," I say. "I like the cracking sound."

"You're sure?" he says.

"I'm here," I say. "We might as well do it."

So he begins.

He holds up my arm and presses a few places on my stomach and chest. Then he sits me up and has me lean back into him, cradling me as he cracks one place in my back. It makes me laugh because it feels like being a baby.

After that he cracks my neck, a loud crack that sends a shiver across my shoulder, down my arm, and out my fingertips.

"The lights are on," he says.

He has me turn over and put my head in the donut so I'm looking at the floor. He presses a little clicky thing on my back.

The chanting in the room gets louder.

"What language is she singing?" I say.

"Your language," Dr. Prem says.

"Mine?"

"Sanskrit."

"I wondered about that," I say.

I relax into the table. My body feels better. My head is quieter.

I feel the tiniest bit happy, like things aren't as bad as I thought they were.

The woman sings in Sanskrit, the language of me.

Dr. Prem finishes the adjustment by asking me to take a deep breath and hold it. He says, "Think about any physical pain or tension in your body."

There's lots of physical pain and tension.

A pain in my neck from Mom.

A pain in my ass from Sweet Caroline.

A pain in my gut from not having a girlfriend.

And a pain somewhere lower that I don't want to talk about.

Dr. Prem says, "Exhale," and I let the pain go.

"Again," he says, and I breathe in and hold it. "This time imagine any emotional distress—worries, fears, upset."

I've got a lot of that, too. Maybe more than a sixteen-year-old should have. I exhale and try to let it go.

"Last time," Dr. Prem says, "the deepest breath yet."

I suck in a long, deep breath.

"You are connected to the Infinite and Divine—" Dr. Prem says.

I'm flooded with a feeling of lightness.

"—with every breath that you take," Dr. Prem says. "Now exhale."

I let the air rush from my lungs. I try to make the big *whoosh* sound that Dr. Prem likes to hear.

That's when it hits me.

A vision.

Maybe that's the wrong name for it. I don't believe in visions. But it's something.

I see me with The Initials, walking hand in hand in a forest.

We walk into a clearing, and Mom is there. She's sitting with a picnic spread out in front of her. A vegetarian cornucopia. The Initials and I join her. We laugh and talk about everything with Mom.

Dad walks by and sits down next to us. He and Mom look at each other—a kind look, not the nasty glances they give each other in real life.

Even Sweet Caroline is there. She comes bounding out of the forest and plops down next to me, jams her hand into a bowl of blue corn chips.

We're all happy in this vision. Together and happy.

And then it dissolves.

I open my eyes.

"Where did you go?" Dr. Prem says.

"I'm not sure."

He touches my shoulder.

"Rest here for a moment."

I lie on the table, exhaling long breaths up towards the ceiling.

Dr. Prem marks something down on my chart. He puts it back in the holder and starts to walk away.

"Do you believe in visions, Dr. Prem?"

"I believe in everything," he says.

I have to change my life.

That's what I write in my journal the next day. It's what I felt after my vision. The gap between my real life and the vision was so great that I have to do something about it. Life as it currently looks does not work for me anymore. I have no choice but to change.

So I come up with a plan.

It starts Monday morning. It starts with school. It starts with telling the truth.

When I get to campus, I go straight to the main office. It's empty except for the Israeli office lady.

"*Boker tov*," she says, tapping away on the computer.

"Good morning to you, too," I say.

She looks up.

"Sanskrit!" she says. She pronounces it correctly this time. She jumps up from her seat and throws her arms around me. Her chest presses against mine. It's much softer than it looks from a distance.

This woman hated me a few days ago, and now she's holding me like her long-lost child. I'm so shocked, I don't know whether to hug her back or run out of the room screaming.

"How are you, *motek*? Oh, where's your *kippah*?"

I touch my head.

"I guess I forgot it."

"Let's get you taken care of."

She reaches into a drawer, pulls out a large crocheted *kippah* that looks like the Israeli flag. I wince as she pops it on my head.

"I need to see the dean," I say.

"Of course. But he's in the cafeteria right now."

"It's really important."

"He wants to see you, too. I know he does. Go right down there."

I extract myself from her hug.

"We're all praying for your mother," she says.

She rubs my back in small circles. It feels kind of nice. I stay there for a second.

"You poor boy," she says. "I'm Dorit, by the way. If you need anything, you come and see Dorit."

"It's a little itchy in the middle, Dorit."

"What's that?"

"My back. It's a little itchy. . . ."

She moves her hand to scratch me low and in the middle where it's hard to reach. She has big nails, unlike my mom, who keeps hers trimmed all the way down for yoga. The nails feel good through my shirt.

"Is that better?" she says.

"Much," I say.

She smiles at me. I consider asking for a shoulder rub, but that seems a little over the top.

"I'll be in the cafeteria," I say.

"He's here!"

Talya Stein shouts when I walk into the cafeteria.

I look behind me to see who she's so excited about.

"Sanskrit!" she says.

It's me.

Normally, I'm not the kind of guy people get excited about seeing. I'm more like the guy in school you don't notice until something bad happens to him. Juvenile cancer or rehab or something. But I guess Mom's fake accident qualifies.

I was expecting to find the dean at an early morning coffee meeting. Instead there is a bunch of students here. When Talya calls my name, a dozen of them turn around and burst into applause. It's not standing ovation applause—more like that slow, steady applause that cheers you on. I hold up my hands to signal them to stop, but they just applaud louder.

I wonder if this is how the guru feels when he walks

into a room. You could get used to this kind of treatment.

"Sorry to interrupt. I'm looking for the dean."

A couple of students point across the cafeteria. The dean is on the far side of the room talking to a girl who has her back to me. I can't see her face, but I recognize her hair right away, tight curls spilling down to her shoulders.

The Initials.

I think of the vision in Dr. Prem's office. The Initials and I were together holding hands.

I have to remind myself that I'm not here to fantasize about The Initials. I'm here to tell the truth.

The dean sees me walking towards him and stops talking. The Initials turns around and her eyes widen.

"Shalom," she says.

"Shalom," I say.

These are the first words we've spoken to each other since second grade. Not the very first words, but the first kind words. We've spoken some *excuse me*s, some *get out of my way*s, some *can I borrow a pencil*s, and other unavoidable school chatter. But we've never greeted each other.

Shalom. Hello, good-bye, and peace—all in one word.

The Initials. Love, pain, and grief—all in two letters.

"Sanskrit," she says.

It's exciting to hear her say my name after all this time.

"Guilty," I say, and I smile.

"We used to go to elementary together."

"We did? I don't remember." Which is the second biggest lie I've told in my life.

"How are you holding up, Aaron?" the dean says.

"Good," I say. Then I look at The Initials and add, "As good as can be expected."

"Of course," he says.

"I need to speak with you for a moment, sir," I say.

He says, "I'm a little embarrassed to be caught with my hand in the cookie jar like this."

"Cookie jar?"

He motions towards the room, the students.

"We're planning a little something," he says. He gives The Initials a nod. "It was the students' idea. Ms. Jacobs presented it to me."

Judi Jacobs. JJ.

The Initials.

"We wanted to do something for your family," she says. "A fund-raiser to help get your mom well."

"You're giving us a telethon?"

She laughs. The dean throws her a look.

"Sorry, that was funny. But seriously, I hope the idea isn't insulting. We just—I mean—the dean said they were keeping your mom down in South Bay—"

"Orange County," the dean says.

"That's right," she says. "And she needs rehabilitation? That's going to cost thousands of dollars."

The dean interrupts.

"He gets the idea, Ms. Jacobs. Understand, Aaron. It's as much for us as it is for you. A way for the school to come together and help a member of our community."

"We're the planning committee," The Initials says. "We wanted to surprise you."

"I'm surprised," I say.

I look around at the assembled students. It's crazy that they're all here for me. Crazy and touching at the same time. How am I going to tell them they're wasting their time?

That's when I notice Barry Goldwasser in the crowd. Mr. One-Minute Mitzvahs himself.

"We're going to get your mom home, no matter what it takes," he says, stepping to the front of the pack. "That's one thing about the Jewish community. We take care of our own."

God, I hate this kid.

"You said you needed to talk to me," the dean says.

"Yes," I say.

"What is it?"

The Initials looks at me. They all do, all these kids who want to help me and my family.

"Another time," I tell the dean.

"Are you sure? We can step out."

"I'm at a loss for words right now."

The students laugh. A nice laugh, like they're on my side. I don't hear a laugh like that very often.

"We'll plan the event for this Thursday night," Barry says. "We'll call it A Night of *Tzedakah* for— What's your mother's name?"

"Rebekah," I say.

"*Tzedakah* for Rebekah. That has a nice ring to it," he says.

Tzedakah. Charity.

"I know you have a lot going on," The Initials says, "but I need a few minutes to ask you some questions about your life. So we can tell people about your family."

The first class tone sounds.

"We'll meet again at lunch, everyone," Barry calls out.

The room starts to clear.

"Dean Shapiro," The Initials says, "I know it's time for class, but would it be alright if I stayed here and did a little work with—"

"Of course," he says.

She smiles. That's when I realize she's talking about me.

And her.

Together.

"You two take all the time you need," the dean says. "I'll let your first-period professors know you'll be late."

Then he goes out and leaves us alone.

"It's been a long time, hasn't it?"

The Initials flips open a yellow pad as she says it. She's businesslike, getting ready for the interview while barely looking at me.

"A long time since when?" I say.

"Since we spoke last," she says.

"I'm not sure how long it's been," I say, even though I know exactly how long.

"We were friends, like, a thousand years ago in second grade."

"That is a long time," I say. "I barely remember."

She looks at her pad.

"Me, neither," she says. She clicks open a pen. "Anyway, I'm sorry to hear about your mom. Is there anything I can do?"

"You're doing it. Thank you."

"How is she? Everyone is wondering."

"You know—"

I stare at the ground as if the thought of Mom's suffering is too painful.

"Say no more," she says. And she smiles. "I'm glad we can help in some small way."

I look at her eyes. They're bright green, dotted with a few speckles of brown. I don't think I've ever looked directly in her eyes. I'm always seeing her from behind or the side, studying different parts of her without really looking at her.

For a moment I consider hugging her, or at least opening my arms to see what happens. Maybe *sick mom* equals *hugs from girls*. If the mean Israeli office lady was scratching my back ten minutes ago, who knows what's possible?

"I've got a ton of questions to ask you," she says.

"Why?"

"The dean wants us to prepare something for him to say."

"Like at a funeral."

"Not at all," she says, horrified.

"I just mean—You know how the rabbi interviews the family before a funeral so he knows what to say?"

I'm thinking about when Zadie died. His rabbi asked if I had any special memories of my grandfather. What I mostly remembered was how my mother complained every weekend when we had to go over to his house. And my father would say, "Zadie bought us this house. We can suck it up for one more Shabbat."

"It's not a funeral," The Initials says. "God forbid."

"I know," I say.

"But you're okay if I ask you some things?"

"Of course."

The Initials looks at her phone.

"Shoot, look how late it is," she says. "I have math first period and Burchstein's a killer."

"Professor Burchstein? That's AP calculus. I didn't know there were juniors in that class."

She shrugs. "I'm pretty good at math. And I'm out of courses after this, so I have to take classes at UCLA next year."

"Impressive."

"Right. Jewish girls who are good at math. Very exciting stuff."

"You guys should have your own calendar. How many of you are there?"

"Just me."

"Do you have twelve good photos?"

She laughs.

"You should get to class," I say. "I mean, we don't want the wrath of Burchstein coming down on you."

"How about if I get your number?" Judi says. "We can meet up someplace later. I mean, if that's okay with you. We've only got a few days to put this whole thing together."

"It's okay with me," I say.

Judi waits.

"Your number?" she says.

I try to think of my phone number, and I can't. Not

with her staring at me. I start to panic, not knowing what I'm going to do. Then I remember that you can look at your phone and check the number in the settings.

I take out my phone while she waits patiently with her own.

"New phone," I say.

"Oh, okay," she says.

The number finally pops up, and I read it to her.

"Thanks, Sanskrit. I'm glad we're having a chance to be of service to you like this. Barry is excited, too."

"Barry?"

"Barry Goldwasser."

"Oh, that Barry."

"He's everywhere, right?"

"Like acne," I say.

"Ouch," she says. "So I'll call you soon."

She walks out, and I stand there, trying to make sense of everything that's just happened.

The plan. I was going to tell the dean the truth.

I could still do it. March upstairs and pull the whole thing down on top of me. But if I do that, The Initials is gone.

No. She's not The Initials anymore.

Judi.

She has a name. We know each other again. She even has my phone number.

If I tell the truth, that's over.

Maybe my plan needs to be adjusted.

I'll get to know Judi better, at least well enough that she understands me. She might even understand why I did what I did. Then when I tell the dean, I'll have someone on my side. And if she's on my side, the students might understand, too. It won't be such a big deal that I lied. It might even be funny to them.

Judi and me, standing together. Almost like my vision.

I just have to give us enough time to remember each other.

"I'm proud of you."

That's what Mom says when I tell her what happened with Dr. Prem. I don't tell her about my vision. But I say that Dr. Prem adjusted me, and I felt a lot better afterwards.

"I knew you would feel better," Mom says. "You fight me on things that I know are good for you. But when you do them, you find out I'm right."

That's when I realize Mom's not really proud of me. She's proud of herself. When I do what she wants and it works out, she feels like a success.

"You're always right, Mom."

"Really?" she says, getting excited.

That's the secret of a good relationship with Mom. I have to be like Herschel's dad, Mr. Weingarten, and go along with everything Mom says. Nodding. It's the key to everything.

But nodding means accepting the guru, watching mom crash and burn and maybe take us down with her.

That's not my vision. My vision is to change my life. To bring my family back together.

You can't have a strange man stay at our house.

That's what I'm going to say to Mom. I'll tell her it's for Sweet Caroline's sake as well as mine. I'll talk about how it's not healthy for a young girl to see those things. No matter that Sweet Caroline is twelve going on forty-seven. She's a kid and she needs positive influences. Preferably ones who don't wear sheets and smell like essential oils.

"We need to talk about the guru," I say.

"He's gone," Mom says with a wave of her hand.

"Gone where?"

"From our house. Don't worry so much, Sanskrit."

"I'm not worried," I say, even though it's not true.

"I have an idea," Mom says.

I brace myself.

Mom + Idea = Danger

"How about we go out to dinner tonight. Just you and me," she says.

"Is this your idea?"

"Who else's idea would it be?"

"I don't know."

"It's a mother-son date. What do the psychologists call it?"

"Quality time?"

"Exactly. I owe you a dinner, and I pay my debts.

Anywhere you'd like to go. As long as they have a vegetarian option."

"What about Sweet Caroline?"

"She's having dinner at a friend's house. What do you think?"

I think I can barely believe it. But I say, "It's a date."

"Why don't you pick a place," Mom says.

I'm thinking I have to keep Mom out of Brentwood if possible. "How about Vegan Glory?"

I choose it because it's over by The Grove, and even though it's fake vegan stuff, it's also fake Thai, which means I have a decent shot at some noodles with peanut sauce, and Mom won't complain.

"Are you sure? I didn't think you liked vegan food," Mom says.

"I like it well enough."

Actually, I hate it. I don't know why I always tell Mom I like it.

Mom smiles. She says, "You won't hear an argument from me. What do you think if we get dressed up a little. Make it special."

Special. I like the way that sounds.

"Do you love beef?"

That's what the waiter says, and he gives us a big wink. I want to ask him why the hell we'd come to Vegan Glory if we loved beef. Then he winks with the other eye. Which makes me think he might have a tic. It's hard to resent a waiter with a tic.

"I hope you love, love, love beef," he says, and winks again, "because tonight's special is Beef Lover's Rainbow."

"A rainbow made of beef? How delicious," I say. "Does it come with a unicorn made of bacon?"

"You're a funny guy," he says.

"This is my son. He has a great sense of humor," my mother says.

"I can hear that," the waiter says.

"Tell us about the beef," Mom says.

"It's not real beef, of course. It's a beef illusion."

"Good, because we're paying with a cash illusion," I say.

Mom laughs. I'm feeling good tonight. I'm dressed up. I'm out with Mom. If you added Dad to the mix, it would be like my vision in Dr. Prem's office.

"Beef or cash, they are both illusory," he says. "Everything that seems solid is not solid at all. That's a Zen principle."

"That's very deep," I say, because I see Mom nodding like she agrees.

"Why don't you order it?" Mom says. And then without even waiting for me, she tells the waiter: "Let's get a beef rainbow for my son."

"Wow," I say. "Okay."

"We'll get the chicken satay, too," Mom says. "And you love noodles, don't you Sanskrit?"

"That's a lot of food, Mom."

Mom waves me off, then turns back to the twitchy waiter. "Peanut noodles. And black rice, too. And could we get the black tofu cod?"

"Impressive," the waiter says.

"My son and I are celebrating," Mom says.

"What are you celebrating?" the waiter says.

"What are we celebrating?" I say.

"Life," Mom says. "The miracle of life. The way it's constantly changing and surprising you."

I'm not sure what Mom is talking about, but I nod and smile like I'm on board with the idea.

"That's really something to celebrate," the waiter says.

"We should celebrate every day, but we don't. We forget," Mom says.

"So true," the waiter says.

He and Mom look at each other like something deep is passing between them.

The waiter goes, and Mom pats the chair beside her.

"Sit next to me," she says.

"Really?" I say.

"Why not?"

I get up and move next to her.

"You've got a lot on your mind," Mom says.

"Oh, no. Is this one of those mom-son talks I've heard so much about?"

"Very funny," she says.

I take a sip of water.

"Talk to me, Sanskrit."

I look at her, trying to see if she really means it. She's in a good mood, so I decide to risk it.

"Do you ever think about Dad?" I say.

"What is there to think about?" she says.

"What happened between you."

"That was a difficult chapter in my life, Sanskrit. And it was a long time ago."

"Not so long."

"I don't understand you. Most kids move on after divorce. I know it was painful for you, but life goes on. Things change."

"Not for me."

"For everyone."

I think about second grade. The Initials. The end of The Initials.

"I hang onto things a long time," I say. "I don't know why."

"It's because you don't believe in anything. How can you surrender your life when you think you're in charge of it?"

I take a sip of water.

"Lots of kids at B-Jew don't believe, and it's not a problem for them."

"You know I don't like when you call it that."

"I'm just saying I'm not the only nonbeliever."

"I'm not asking you to believe what they teach you at school. I just think you should believe in something greater than you."

"But why?"

Mom thinks about it.

"Well, for one thing, not believing really bothers you."

I don't say anything.

"Why do you think that is?" Mom says.

I shrug. Is Mom right? I'm not sure.

"You could talk to the guru about it," Mom says.

"Why did you have to bring him up?"

"He's a spiritual leader. Maybe he could be a resource for you."

"I go to Jewish school. I've got plenty of resources."

Real resources, I think. *Not self-proclaimed resources.*

Before Mom can say anything else, we're interrupted by a plate of chicken satay.

I look at skewers of something that approximates chicken, complete with a thick peanut sauce to dip it in. It may be fake, but it's also fried. Everything tastes good when it's fried, even crappy vegetarian food. It's the most democratic of the cooking processes.

Mom bows her head. I wait for her to finish praying or whatever it is she does, and then I dig in.

"I'm glad we have some time together," Mom says as she attacks her skewer.

"Me, too," I say. "Especially without Sweet Caroline."

"That's not nice."

"I didn't mean it like that," I say.

I remind myself to be careful about telling the truth. Most of the time Mom doesn't like it.

The rest of the food arrives. Steaming sticky rice, a giant platter of peanut noodles, and the beef rainbow dish, which neither looks like beef nor rainbow. Finally, the waiter brings out a giant tofu patty shaped like a smiling fish.

"What's he smiling about?" I say. "We're going to eat him."

Mom laughs, but then she stops suddenly and looks over my shoulder. Her eyes widen.

"What are the chances?" she says.

I turn around.

The guru is walking into Vegan Glory.

At first I'm stunned. I can't believe he's here, all the way on the east side of town. Then I think we're in a popular vegan place, so it's not so surprising. Then I think something else, but I push that out of my head.

Mom jumps up, smiling.

The guru sees us and comes over. He's dressed in clean, bright blue sheets, beaming his guru smile. He looks like a happy load of laundry.

"*Namaste*," Mom says, giving him a bow, her hands pressed in front of her chest.

"*Namaste*," the guru says. "Dear Rebekah. And dear Sanskrit."

"I'm not your dear," I say. "And neither is my mom."

"It's an honorific," the guru says, but with his accent, it's a little hard to understand him. It sounds like a combination of *horror* and *terrific*.

Terrific horror. Welcome to my world.

"What a surprise," Mom says.

She's smiling so hard, it looks like she's wearing a mask. Happy Mom mask.

"A surprise, yes," the guru says. But he doesn't seem surprised at all.

There's an awkward moment with the three of us standing over a table full of food. Then Mom says, "Would you like to join us, guru? You don't mind, do you, Sanskrit?"

"It doesn't thrill me," I say.

They both look at me.

I think about walking out of the restaurant without a word. Slamming the door behind me like I did in the gym the other night.

Then I remember we're far from home, all the way on Beverly and La Cienega near The Grove. I could take a bus home. But nobody takes the bus in L.A. Correction: lots of people take the bus, but not a lot of kids in Brentwood. I curse myself for not knowing how the buses work. I could call a cab, but that would be like thirty dollars or more. I'd have to ask Mom to borrow money before I stormed out. That would sort of ruin the gesture.

In other words, I'm stuck.

"Sanskrit. May I join you?" the guru says.

Is he really asking, or is he just being polite? I look at Mom with her happy mask still on.

"Fine," I say.

"Good," he says, "Because I am famished."

Mom calls for an extra place setting for the guru. People around the restaurant are looking at us. You don't often see a man dressed head to toe in blue in Los Angeles. Not unless he's panhandling on the Walk of Fame.

The waiter with the twitch comes back to the table. He takes one look at the guru and bows deeply.

"Guru Bharat!" he whispers.

"Please," the guru says, gesturing for him to rise.

"What an honor," the waiter says, and winks three times. "What brings you to our humble restaurant?"

"Hunger," the guru says.

"That is so profound," the waiter says.

The waiter puts down a fork and backs away.

"You must get that a lot," Mom says.

"Misunderstanding?" the guru says. "Yes, I get it a lot. Don't we all?"

"Amen," I say.

Mom throws me a warning look.

"Let's eat before it gets cold," Mom says.

She looks at the guru, whose head is bowed.

"Wait," she says to me, and I pause with a chicken skewer halfway in my mouth while the guru prays.

It goes on for a long time—so long that my mouth starts to water. Finally, the guru looks up. I chew.

The guru pulls up his long sleeves and digs into the tofu fish.

"Tell me about yourself, Sanskrit," he says.

I'm still holding the skewer in my hand. I think about poking him in the eye with it.

"Nothing to tell," I say.

"Sanskrit goes to Jewish school," Mom says.

"The religion of your birth," the guru says to Mom.

"You remember," Mom says.

"I remember everything from our chats," the guru says.

Mom giggles and puts her hand on the guru's fore-arm. The fake chicken churns in my stomach.

"How do you feel about being Jewish?" the guru asks me.

"I love it," I say.

"He does not love it," Mom says.

"Sure I do. We invented the bagel. How can you not love that?"

"I wish you would tell the truth," Mom says.

Her hand is still on the guru's arm.

I stare at it.

I look at Mom—her makeup, the way she's taken her hair down into two loose pigtails, the white dress with blue stitching that she never wears.

"I wish you would tell the truth, too," I say.

"What are you talking about?" Mom says.

"You planned this. This whole coincidence. It's not a coincidence at all."

"That's not true," Mom says.

"It's more than true," I say. "And I'm sick of pre-tending it's not."

I pull at my button-down shirt. A minute ago it felt good on me, but now it feels scratchy, foreign.

"Don't lie to him," the guru says.

"Don't tell me what to do," Mom says.

"Don't lie to me, Mom," I say.

Mom gives the guru an angry look. The same kind she used to give Dad.

"Fine. You want the truth?" Mom says. "I wanted you two to have a chance to get to know each other, so you would like each other."

"Why do we need to like each other?" I say.

Mom and the guru share a look. Mom nods to him.

"Your mother and I started a relationship as friends—" the guru says.

"I don't want to hear this," I say.

"—but something has happened between us," he says. "Something beautiful."

Mom's hand slides down his forearm to his fingers. They intertwine.

I stand up and throw my napkin on the table.

"You set me up," I say to Mom.

"Please, Sanskrit. We're trying to share good news with you," Mom says.

"What's good about it?" I say. I fling down my fork, and a chunk of tofu meat goes flying.

I storm out to the sound of Mom apologizing—not to me—to the guru.

I'm going away.

That's what I think as I walk around the neighborhood. I can handle this because I'm going away soon. One more year, really a year and a half, and then I'll be at Brandeis. Away from this place, away from Brentwood, away from my crazy family.

Away from Mom.

The thought upsets me, and then I get angry at myself for being upset. What kind of a baby is afraid to leave his mother? Kids are supposed to want to leave home, especially homes like mine.

I try to imagine myself all the way on the other side of the country at Brandeis. I wonder if Mom will miss me. I wonder if she'll think of me at all.

Out of sight, out of mind.

Just like God.

All of Judaism is based on remembering God, reaching out to him, asking for his help. Reminding ourselves of him at every moment.

Why do we have to do all that work?

Because God's not here in the first place.

If God were here, there would be no need for religion. We wouldn't have to remember him or honor him. We'd come out of our houses in the morning, and God would be sitting on a cloud with a lightning bolt in one hand and a Starbucks in the other.

You'd say, "Good morning, God. How did I do yesterday?"

If you were good, you'd get the Starbucks. If you were bad—

You'd get the guru.

I walk a big circle in the neighborhood around the restaurant. By the time I head back, Mom's car isn't in the parking lot anymore. I'm thinking that maybe she left, when a horn beeps.

Mom pulls up, her tire scraping the curb. The guru is sitting next to her in front.

"We're going home," Mom says through her open window.

"Who's we?"

"You and I. We'll drop off Guru Bharat first."

"Good," I say. And I get in the car.

"You're awfully quiet."

We're sitting at a stoplight after dropping off the guru. I'm in the backseat, and I haven't said a word.

"I'm trying to communicate with you like Sweet Caroline's psychologist said I should," Mom says.

The light turns green. There's a beep behind us.

"Sanskrit," Mom says. "Nobody can plan for love. It's mysterious."

Another beep.

If I open my mouth, I'll say something terrible, so I keep it closed. I feel the anger churning in my stomach, a cement mixer filled with fake beef products.

"Sanskrit," Mom says.

A long horn blast.

Mom steps on the gas, and we're moving again.

"I give up," she says.

Me, too, I think.

When we get home, Mom pulls into the driveway but doesn't open the garage door.

"I'm taking a drive," she says.

Mom never takes drives. She's too concerned with leaving a small carbon footprint. But tonight she leaves the car running and waits for me to get out. Then she pulls out of the driveway fast, narrowly missing our mailbox before disappearing into the night.

"Where's Mom going?"

Sweet Caroline is standing inside the door when I get inside. I can tell she's been watching through the front window.

"How do I know?" I say.

"She never drives at night."

For all Mom's spiritual work, she's scared of a lot of things. Night driving, sugar, cell phones, the laser scanner at the grocery store, which she thinks can cause blindness despite the fact we have yet to meet a blind cashier.

"Did something happen at dinner?" Sweet Caroline says.

"I don't want to talk about it."

I storm past her, heading for my room.

"Don't blame me for your messed-up relationship," she says.

"Screw you, Caroline," I shout behind me.

"Sweet!" she shouts after me.

I slam my bedroom door closed. Then I open and slam it again. The wood shivers in the frame.

I hear an answering slam from down the hall. Then another. Then a third.

Jewish Morse code.

I pace around my room, making small, angry circles. I get angrier and angrier until I'm ready to explode. I pull out my journal.

I flip through it until I find my last entry.

I have to change my life.

That's what it says.

I can check that one off the list. It's changed for the worse.

I turn to a blank page.

I write:

G—D

Then I cross it out. I write:

HaShem

"You can always talk to *HaShem*," Herschel once said. "He's omnipresent."

I said, "That's like those reality shows where they have cameras everywhere, even in the bathroom. The ACLU should object to an omnipresent God."

"Omnipresent means we have a constant companion. We're never really alone because we have God beside us."

I look at the word *HaShem* written on the page in front of me. I imagine him here with me in the room.

I don't believe it. I cross out his name.

I write:

DEAR MOM,
   I HATE YOU.

I tear that out of the journal and crunch it up. I toss it in the trash. Then I take it out and rip it into tiny pieces and throw those out.

I start a new page in the journal.

DEAR MOM,
   I HAVE A LOT OF THINGS I WANT TO SAY TO YOU.
   I HATE YOU.
   THIS IS THE TRUTH.
   I HATE YOU MORE THAN ANYTHING. I HOPE YOU GET INTO A CAR ACCIDENT TONIGHT WHILE YOU'RE DRIVING WHEREVER YOU'RE DRIVING. IF YOU EVER READ THIS, YOU'RE PROBABLY GOING TO SAY, OH, HE JUST SAID THAT BECAUSE HE WAS ANGRY.

BUT IT'S NOT BECAUSE I'M ANGRY. IT'S BECAUSE IT'S TRUE.

I DON'T CARE IF YOU NEVER COME HOME AGAIN.

IT WOULD BE EASIER ON ME. BECAUSE IF YOU GOT INTO AN ACCIDENT, I WOULD KNOW I'D LOST YOU AND I WOULDN'T EXPECT ANYTHING FROM YOU. IT'S NOT LIKE YOU CAN WANT STUFF FROM DEAD PEOPLE. AND EVERYONE AT SCHOOL WILL MOURN WITH ME FOR REAL, AND I WON'T HAVE TO ADMIT I'M A LIAR.

BUT UNFORTUNATELY YOU'RE ALIVE, AND ALL YOU DO IS HURT ME.

YOU INVITED ME TO DINNER TONIGHT. I THOUGHT IT WAS ABOUT YOU AND ME, AND IT TURNS OUT IT WAS ALL A SETUP. IT WAS REALLY JUST A DINNER FOR YOU TO BE CLOSER TO YOUR GURU. OR FOR YOU TO TRY TO MAKE ME LOVE YOUR GURU LIKE YOU DO, AND THAT'S BULLSHIT. YOU CAN'T TRICK PEOPLE LIKE THAT. YOU CAN'T TRICK YOUR SON.

I'm so angry as I write this, I want to break the pen and stab it into something.

I bend the pen until it's on the brink of snapping, but I stop before it does. I go back to the page.

> I DON'T WANT YOU TO BE MY MOTHER ANYMORE. YOU'RE NOT GOOD AT IT. YOU'RE GOOD AT OTHER THINGS, BUT NOT AT THIS. YOU'RE A GOOD YOGA TEACHER, FOR INSTANCE. I GIVE YOU THAT MUCH. YOU'RE GOOD AT TEACHING YOGA, AND I'M SORRY I'M NOT GOOD AT LEARNING IT BECAUSE YOU'VE TRIED TO HELP ME AND I KNOW I'VE LET YOU DOWN. BUT I DON'T WANT YOU TO THINK YOU'RE A BAD TEACHER BECAUSE I'M NOT ABLE TO DO ADVANCED MOVES.
> I'M JUST SAYING THERE ARE THINGS THAT WE EXCEL AT AND THINGS THAT WE DON'T.
> YOU DON'T EXCEL AT BEING MY MOTHER.

I'm afraid to write this. It's hard to tell the truth about how I feel, even when it's just on paper. I decide I'm going to write the letter, then throw it out. I'm never giving it to Mom. I'll write it and destroy it. That's what a journal is, right? It's a private place for me to have my feelings. So I'm going to say what I have to say. I'm going to let it all out.

I go back to the page, write a few more words, and the pen runs out of ink.

I throw it across the room. I search through my backpack, but I can only find a red pen.

SORRY THE COLOR OF INK JUST CHANGED, BUT MY PEN RAN OUT AND I HAVE TO USE A DIFFERENT PEN. THAT'S ANOTHER THING I HATE ABOUT YOU, MOM. I SHOULD HAVE A COOL LAPTOP LIKE OTHER KIDS. I SHOULDN'T BE USING A PEN AT ALL. THAT'S TECHNOLOGY FROM HUNDREDS OF YEARS AGO. DO YOU KNOW HOW MANY KIDS HAVE THEIR OWN LAPTOPS IN SCHOOL NOW? ALL OF THEM. THEY DON'T HAVE ONE STUPID NETBOOK THEY HAVE TO SHARE WITH THEIR WHOLE FAMILY.

That's why I haven't seen our netbook for so long. It's been in Mom's room so she can use it to chat with the guru. That thought makes me angry all over again.

I'M TIRED OF THINKING ABOUT THIS, MOM.
I'M TIRED OF TRYING WITH YOU.
I GIVE UP.
I'M DONE.

I'M NOT YOUR SON ANYMORE.
THAT'S THE TRUTH.

MAYBE YOU'LL BE RELIEVED WHEN YOU READ THIS, OR MAYBE YOU'LL BE UPSET, OR MAYBE YOU'LL BE NOTHING AT ALL. IF YOU READ IT AND YOU WANT TO TALK TO ME ABOUT IT, I MIGHT BE WILLING TO DO THAT.

JUST READ THIS AND THINK ABOUT IT. OKAY?

I close the journal. My hand is shaking and I'm sweating.

I lie back in bed and put the journal on my stomach.

I think about dinner, about the guru walking in, about Mom's happy mask.

I think about the guru in our kitchen the other morning.

I think about how it made me feel.

That's when I decide I'm going to give Mom the letter.

She needs to know the truth.

I carefully tear it out of the journal and fold it up. I don't have any envelopes in my room, but I know Mom keeps some in the kitchen drawer for when she has to send bills.

I sneak out of my room and head for the kitchen.

"You can't eat anything," Sweet Caroline calls from her bedroom.

"I'm not eating," I say from the hall.

Sweet Caroline is being a bitch because I yelled at her before.

I swear to God, I would kill for a house with real walls. The Jews might have been slaves in Egypt, but I'll bet the walls were thick. Those Egyptian stones were heavy. I wouldn't mind being a slave if it got Sweet Caroline off my back.

"It's after eight and you're heading for the kitchen," Sweet Caroline says through her door. "You know the rules. If you eat, I'll tell Mom."

"Good luck finding her."

"What's that mean?"

"It means she left home and I doubt she's coming back."

There's a pause and then Sweet Caroline's door opens.

She steps out in pink sweats and a T-shirt. The sweats have a picture of Hello Kitty on the butt. One of Mom's yoga ladies gives her old clothes to Sweet Caroline. That's Brentwood. A forty-year-old woman and a twelve-year-old girl are roughly the same size.

"You said she was taking a drive," Sweet Caroline says.

"Since when does she take drives? She's got the carbon footprint of a Brussels sprout."

"What are you saying?"

"Did you notice a man in sheets at breakfast the other day? Do you think it's strange that Mom is nowhere to be found at ten o'clock at night?"

"So?" she says.

"You're blind."

"I'm not blind."

"We went to dinner tonight, and he was there. Mom invited him without telling me."

"Why?"

"They wanted to break the news to me. It's bad, Sweet Caroline. Much worse than we thought."

Sweet Caroline pulls at her eyebrow. She plucks one of the hairs out and rubs it between her fingers.

"Mom's had other creepy boyfriends. Why do you hate this one so much?" she says.

"I don't like how Mom is around him."

"Happy?"

"Brainwashed."

She goes to the kitchen trash and drops the hair into it. She claps her hands together like she's completed an important mission.

"He's going back to India, Sanskrit."

Sweet Caroline reaches into a gift basket for some caramel walnut clusters. She tears the package with her teeth.

"That's how I know we're going to be okay," she says. "He doesn't live in this country."

"You might be right."

"See? I'm not blind."

"Maybe not," I say.

She scrapes chocolate from the roof of her mouth with a finger. Then she goes down the hall to her bedroom.

As much as I hate her, I have to admit she's a pretty brilliant kid. But she's still just a kid.

I know better. I have to protect us. I have to wake Mom up.

I open the drawer where Mom keeps the envelopes. Of course she's out of envelopes.

I see a stack of bills on the counter. I pick out one that Mom hasn't opened yet. Her philosophy is that you don't open bills until they turn red. Before that, it's like eating fruit that's not ripe.

This bill is still black, so I know she's not going to miss it.

I take a steak knife from the drawer and slit the envelope open on the side. Then I slip the bill out and throw it away. I write:

To: Mom
From: Your son

I slide the letter into the envelope so the writing fits into the transparent square.

I go back down the hall, open Mom's door, and slip inside.

I remember when I was a little kid and I'd go into her room in the middle of the night, only then it was *their* room, my parents' room. They tried to send me back to bed, but sometimes I would beg enough that they'd let me stay. I'd snuggle in next to Mom, feel her softness against my back. Mom wasn't skinny and yoga-body hard back then. She had a human body that could give you comfort. Now she's all angles and muscles.

I sit on the edge of her bed, arrange her pillows so they're not a mess, and I lay the envelope on top.

I catch a scent of Mom's shampoo on the pillow. It smells good to be close to her. Not a whiff of her passing by, but pure Mom, concentrated. It makes me feel like a child being carried, my face buried in her neck.

Suddenly, I feel exhausted.

It's like everything that's been happening over the last week fills my body until I can't move. I lie down on Mom's bed and close my eyes. Maybe I fall asleep for a minute, but my eyes snap open again.

I can't be in here when Mom gets home.

I drag myself up from the bed, make sure the envelope is still there, and I go back to my bedroom and wait for Mom to come home.

"Wake up."

I don't even remember falling asleep. I was up nearly the entire night, waiting for the front door to open, for Mom's footsteps in the hall, waiting for her to see the letter, waiting for what might come after.

"Sanskrit?" The voice says.

It's not Mom. It's Sweet Caroline.

"Get up," she says.

She's standing in the half-open doorway.

"What do you want?" I say.

"It's Mom."

"What about her?"

"She didn't come home last night."

"The letter—" I start to say, but I stop myself. It's none of Sweet Caroline's business.

"Mom wrote a letter?" Sweet Caroline says.

"No."

"You said a letter—"

"I was dreaming it," I say.

I sit up fast in bed. It's six on Tuesday morning.

I rub my eyes, trying to wake up.

"How do you know Mom didn't come home?" I say. "Maybe she had an early class."

"Her bed is still made. I'm worried, Sanskrit."

I'm worried, too. Mom has done a lot of irresponsible things, but staying out all night isn't one of them.

"I think we should call the police," Sweet Caroline says.

"You have to calm down," I say.

"I am calm. That's why I think we should call the police."

"Bad idea. They've already got the Child Protective Services report because of you."

"That was a long time ago. And it got discredited, remember?"

"My point is if the police find out Mom didn't come home, things could get complicated."

Sweet Caroline thinks about it, biting at a nail. Mom clicks her nails on her teeth when she's worried, but Sweet Caroline bites until she bleeds.

"This is a crisis. We need to call Dad," she says.

"That's the worst time to call Dad."

Dad's idea of a crisis is having to make dinner on a weeknight.

"Why don't you call the yoga studio just to make sure she's not there," I say.

"What will you do?"

"I'll check the house."

"Don't leave, Sanskrit."

"I'm not leaving. I'm going down the hall."

"I'll come with you."

"Stay here and call the yoga studio. I swear I'll be right back."

Sweet Caroline stretches out her arms like she's going to reach for me, but she doesn't. It's funny how she's so tough and so vulnerable at the same time. She gets scared and suddenly she wants a big brother.

I wait for Sweet Caroline to get on her phone, and I head down the hall.

I slip into Mom's room.

It's dark. I crack open the blinds, and light floods in.

I look at her pillow.

The letter is gone.

I check between the sheets and under the bed, just in case it fell. Then I look back at the pillow.

Gone.

Does that mean Mom came home and found it?

I rush back into the living room.

"Your wife has disappeared," Sweet Caroline is saying into the phone.

"Hang up."

"It's our father," she says, holding her hand over the receiver. "I'm informing him of current events."

She speaks into the phone: "I don't know where she went, Daddy. I just know she never came home."

I hear Dad's voice coming through the earpiece.

"You have to come and get us," Sweet Caroline says. "We'll find Mom and then you can drive us to school."

Dad's voice again.

"An hour's too long!" Sweet Caroline says.

She looks at me, desperate.

What can I say? Everything is difficult for Dad. That's why we don't call him when it's not his weekend.

Sweet Caroline thinks for a second, then she says into the phone, "You have two unsupervised, unfed children here. What if the big one happens and we have no water in the house?"

Dad says something, then Sweet Caroline puts down the phone.

"He'll be over in five minutes," she says.

"That was mean of you," I say.

"Desperate times call for desperate measures," she says.

"How could she just leave you here alone?"

Dad says it like he's angry, like parents should be responsible for their children at all times. That's easy for him to say when he only has to be responsible one weekend a month.

"That's why we called you," Sweet Caroline says. "It's weird of her."

"Have you checked all her usual haunts?" Dad says. "Runyon Canyon, the yoga center, that colon cleansing place . . ."

"Gross, daddy."

"It's not my fault. Your mother is nuts now," he says.

Sweet Caroline clamps her hands over her ears.

"You married her," I say. "You must have seen something in her."

"People change," Dad says.

He's looking at Mom's altar as he says it. There's

a little picture of Guru Bharat on the table next to a candle. I never noticed it before.

"Maybe they can change back," I say.

"Why are we standing here talking about unimportant things?" Sweet Caroline says.

Dad sighs. "You're right," he says. "Let's take a ride and see what we can see."

"Someone has to stay here," I say.

"Why?" Sweet Caroline says.

"What if Mom comes back and nobody knows it, and we're still out there looking for her."

"She'll call us," Sweet Caroline says.

"Good point," Dad says.

"She lost her phone," I say.

"Really? That's a problem," Dad says.

"I'll stay and you guys go. Then if something happens, we can call each other."

Sweet Caroline looks at me, trying to figure out if I'm up to something.

"I don't know about this—" Dad says.

"I'm an adult," I say.

Sweet Caroline opens her mouth to say something.

"Practically an adult," I say, cutting her off.

"Alright then," Dad says. "It's you and me, Sweet Pea."

He heads for the car with Sweet Caroline at his heels.

Once they're gone, I pace the house. I sort through

the gift baskets, eating various chocolates.

I check my phone, making sure the ringer is on so I'll hear it.

I pace some more.

Eventually, I end up in my bedroom. I lie down and stare at the ceiling.

I don't know how much time passes before I hear the front door open. I'm thinking they must have found Mom.

"Sweet Caroline?" I call out.

There's no answer.

I hear footsteps in the hall. Mom's door opens and closes.

"Mom?" I say.

Still no answer. I try her door. It's locked.

I hear crying inside her bedroom.

"Can we talk, Mom?"

I feel like I'm outside of my body. I'm dizzy and cold.

"Mom?"

She won't answer me.

I walk into the living room and lay down on her meditation mat. I can feel the indentation of her body from laying on it so many times.

One time when we were still a family, Dad took us up to Mammoth Lake during the winter. Zadie refused to come. He said he spent his childhood running in the woods and saw no reason to repeat the experience.

I still remember that trip. We stayed in a cabin, and I touched snow for the first time. Mom was raised on the East Coast, and she told us stories about the snow when she was a little kid. One night there was a big snowstorm, and Mom got us all to go outside the next morning.

"Watch this!" she said.

She lay back in a snowbank and waved her arms up and down by her sides and scissored her legs open and closed. She hopped out of the indentation so she wouldn't damage it.

"I made a snow angel," Mom said.

I looked at the indentation and I saw what she meant.

Dad lifted up Sweet Caroline and me and laid us in the indentation. We both fit perfectly, curled together in Mom's impression in the snow.

That was a long time ago. Mom and Dad loved each other then. At least it felt like they did.

I settle against the impression in Mom's meditation mat. It's shallow, hard, barely there. I try to fit my body into it, but we don't match anymore.

"Sanskrit."

Mom looks at me from the hallway. Her face is puffy and red. She blows her nose into a tissue.

"I thought you'd still be asleep," Mom says. "I'd get home and you wouldn't even know I'd been gone all night."

I glance at the clock in the kitchen.

"It's eight thirty, Mom. We've been up for two and a half hours."

"I lost track of time," she says. "Where's your sister?"

"With Dad."

"Your father is in the house?"

Dad's not allowed to come in without Mom's permission. The judge told him it's not his house anymore, even if his father was the one who bought it.

"He's driving around looking for you with Sweet Caroline. She called him because we were worried. You didn't come home last night."

"I did come home," she says.

It seems like she's going to sit next to me on her mat, but she doesn't. She goes into the kitchen and leans against the counter.

"I came home after my drive and I found your letter," she says. "At first I was shocked. All those hurtful things you said. I was confused. But the guru helped me understand."

"You saw the guru?"

"I went to see him, and we talked all night."

"What did you talk about?"

"You."

"I don't like you talking about our family with strangers."

"He's not a stranger. I trust him. We have a connection."

"How can you have a connection? You just met him."

"Some day you'll have a connection with a woman, and you'll understand what it's like."

I try to imagine telling Judi everything about me—the problems with Mom and my feelings about Sweet Caroline and my father. It seems impossible to share that stuff with another person.

"He helped me to understand you," Mom says. "And to figure out what I should do."

Mom comes over and sits across from me on the floor.

"Sanskrit, you said I've been a bad mother to you."

"Not bad," I say.

"That's what you said in the letter. Is it the truth?"

I'm so uncomfortable, I can barely sit still.

"Is it?" she says.

"Yes."

I brace for Mom to get angry, but she doesn't. She just nods her head.

"The guru told me I needed to be a hundred percent honest with you. Like you were honest with me."

She closes her eyes and takes a breath.

"Here it is: I try to be a good mother, but I fall short. Sometimes I want to be better and I don't know how, and sometimes I don't want to be better. Sometimes I wonder why I'm a mother in the first place."

"You're a mother because you had kids."

"There was a lot going on when I had you. Family pressure—"

"I don't want to hear this."

"You need to hear it. You're suffering because of it. Because of my bad choices. Your letter made that clear. At first I was angry that you would even talk to me like that, but then I realized you were right."

I try to change my position on the mat. My legs are falling asleep, my thighs numb and tingling.

"Your letter woke me up, Sanskrit."

"I wrote it when I was really angry—"

"The truth was too painful for me to look at on my own. You helped me, Sanskrit. The guru said that your name was more than just a name. Maybe I knew before you were born that you were going to bring me the message I needed to hear, and that's why I called you Sanskrit."

"How would he know?"

"Oh, sweetie," she says.

Mom leans towards me, legs crossed, her hands on her thighs. She can stay in this position for hours. Maybe even days.

"I have to do better. I have to be a real mother to you."

"I'd like that."

"But how can I love you, when I don't love myself?"

"What does that mean?"

"If I don't learn to love myself, I can never be the

kind of mother I want to be. The guru explained that to me."

"You're saying you want to be a good mother?"

"More than anything," Mom says.

She scoots closer, her knees against my knees.

"That's why I'm leaving," she says. "The guru is going back to India, and I'm going with him."

"How does that make you a good mother?"

"This might be hard for you to understand at your age, but I've put everything else in my life first. It's time for me to put *me* first. My happiness. My joy."

"This doesn't make any sense."

"The guru is my chance at happiness. There's real love between us. A spiritual love, not like I've had in the past. It's a new start for me, Sanskrit. "

"Wait—What about us?"

"That's why I need to talk to your father. You're going to live with him while I'm away."

"That's impossible. He can't even keep a plant alive."

"Sweet Caroline told me he has a cactus."

"He lives in an apartment!"

"A nice apartment."

"You've never seen it!" I say.

"It will bring you and your sister closer."

"Who wants that? Mom, this is crazy."

Mom stands up and crosses her arms over her chest.

"I'm shocked that I'm getting such flack from you. I thought you'd be happy for me."

"Why would I be happy?"

"I'm doing it for you," she says. "Because of your letter."

"But I didn't mean what I said. It was just angry stuff. You know how people get angry sometimes and say things they don't mean? That's what the letter was."

"I know that's not true."

I can't think straight. My head is going a mile a minute.

"When are you leaving?" I say.

"In a week," she says.

She reaches out and puts a hand on my chest. My heart chakra or whatever she calls it. She keeps her hand there like she's trying to comfort me. But it just feels like she's pushing me away.

"One week," I say.

"Yes," Mom says with a smile.

"My life is just beginning."

That's what Mom says to Dad. He sways on his feet like he's been hit.

Sweet Caroline stands to the side, rubbing tears from her eyes.

Mom just broke the news to them, and they look like they've been in a car accident.

"'My life is just beginning'? What kind of statement is that?" Dad says.

"An honest one," Mom says.

I watch from behind the kitchen counter. I duck down a little so one of the gift baskets is in the way. My family is less painful when viewed through cellophane and foreign chocolate.

"You're forty-one years old. Your life has been going on for a long time," Dad says. "We had a marriage. We had children."

"*Have* children," I say. "We're still here."

"Of course you are," Dad says.

"What about my bat mitzvah?" Sweet Caroline says.

"Oh, that's right," Mom says, like she just remembered Sweet Caroline is getting bat mitzvahed in the fall. "I'm sure I'll be back for that."

"You don't sound sure," Sweet Caroline says, biting at a nail.

"This is a new chapter for me," Mom says. "I don't understand why I can't get a little support from the people around me."

"Because it makes no sense!" Dad says.

"I don't expect someone whose life has been on hold for twenty years to understand."

"That's a low blow," Dad says.

"It's true," Mom says. "Your father wouldn't fund your start-up, and you crumbled."

"That's not how it happened," Dad says.

But that is how it happened, at least as I understand it. Dad refused to work for Zadie's terry company and tried to get Zadie to fund his tech start-up instead. Zadie refused, saying it was a big waste of money. Dad has spent his life trying to prove him wrong.

"Please stop fighting," Sweet Caroline says.

"We're not fighting," Mom says. "Nothing to fight about. I've already made up my mind."

"So you're leaving your children?" Dad says.

Mom twists her head around, doing the neck rolls that help her relieve stress.

"I'm not leaving them. I'm finding myself," Mom says. "Do I have to remind you they have a father to take care of them while I'm gone?"

"I'm not happy about this," Dad says.

"I don't need you to be happy," Mom says. "I need you to take some responsibility."

"Don't talk to me about responsibility," Dad says. "You won't like what I have to say."

"What do you have to say?"

Dad glances towards us.

"Not now," he says.

"Now is a perfect time," Mom says. "Let's get it all out in the open."

"I'm not the one who destroyed this family. That's all I'm saying."

"What do you mean?" I say. I was there the day the divorce papers showed up. Divorce papers from Dad. "What's he talking about, Mom?"

Mom doesn't answer.

"That's all I'm saying," Dad repeats, looking at Mom.

There's silence in the room. Sweet Caroline sniffles and rubs her nose with her sleeve.

I look towards Mom, still waiting for an answer.

None comes.

"Fine," Dad says. "You need to go off on some insane escapade to India? I can take care of the kids for a little while. I'll move into the house."

"Not the house," Mom says. "I'm subletting the house out to the yoga center."

"No!" Sweet Caroline says.

"Why would you sublet?" Dad says.

"Because I need the income, Joseph, and you can't give it to me."

"But we can't live at Dad's place," Sweet Caroline says. "It's too small."

"Where will they stay?" Dad says. "I've got my workshop."

"You can't clean out a bedroom for your own children?"

"I've only got two of them," Dad says.

"In India, two full families could live in that apartment," Mom says.

"That's why I don't live in India!" Dad says. "And I don't crap in a hole in the ground, or whatever they do over there."

Sweet Caroline slides over and pulls me down the hall, all the way into her bedroom. Mom and Dad continue to argue behind us.

Sweet Caroline closes her door.

"We're dead," she says.

She looks at me, fear in her eyes. She's not often afraid, so it freaks me out a little.

"I was right about Mom," I say. "You see that now."

"You were right," she says.

It's sad that the one time I get my sister to admit

I'm right is the one time I don't want to be.

"She doesn't even care about my bat mitzvah," Sweet Caroline says.

"Maybe that's not such a bad thing," I say, remembering my own bar mitzvah after the divorce. The two sides of our family were so far apart and angry, Herschel said I should have hired Henry Kissinger as a party planner.

"I'll kill myself if we have to live at Dad's," she says.

She slumps down on her bed, biting savagely at a nail.

The Israeli rhythmic gymnastics team looks down at her, a pyramid of smiles.

"I thought you liked Dad."

"I love him. But I don't want to live with him. That would be terrible."

"What's so terrible?"

"Who's going to do the laundry? Who will buy us clothes?"

"Dad, I guess."

"Come on, Sanskrit. He's been wearing the same khakis since 2003."

Mom might be distracted, but at least she keeps the house running. Dad's apartment looks like a scene from a hoarding show. Zadie's house was the same way, only with more expensive junk. They say that's common among survivors. They lost everything once, so they refuse to throw anything away now.

"He's not a good father, Sanskrit. You know this."

She pulls off a chunk of nail, wincing as she draws blood.

I say, "You never talk like that. I wasn't sure we were even living in the same family."

"I don't mean all the time," Sweet Caroline says. "He's a good weekend father when he only has to have fun with us and make sure we're not kidnapped. But he's not good with the other stuff."

"Neither is Mom," I say.

"That's true," Sweet Caroline says. "But we know how to work around her."

Dad shouts in the other room, "My place is too small!"

"So get a job and buy a bigger place!" Mom says.

I wince. It's painful to hear them cutting at each other like this. It reminds me of why they got divorced in the first place. At least why I thought they got divorced. Now I'm not so sure.

Sweet Caroline is looking at a gymnastics poster, tracing the pattern of a girl's leotard.

"What are we going to do?" she says.

"I think I have a plan," I say.

Sweet Caroline looks at me, hopeful for the first time.

"Maybe we can keep Mom here," I say.

"You can't convince her," Sweet Caroline says.

"You know how Mom gets when she makes up her mind about something."

"I don't need to convince her. I need to convince him."

"Dad?"

"The guru."

"I want to talk man-to-man."

The guru is sitting on a meditation mat when I say it. He's alone in the small yoga room in the back of the Center. He doesn't open his eyes or even flinch. If I didn't know better, I'd think he was expecting me.

"An excellent idea," he says.

"In private," I say, and I close the door behind me.

This is what I told Sweet Caroline I'd do. Tell the guru to back off and leave Mom alone. It's probably what I should have done in the first place, but I was too afraid.

"We will talk," the guru says with his eyes still closed, "but I think of it a little differently. I see us less as man-to-man, and more as spiritual being to spiritual being."

"I'm not interested in word games," I say. "I talked to my mom. I know you're planning to take her away."

"*Sanskrit*. I like to say your name. It gives me joy. As it does your mother."

"She likes to say my name?"

"She gave you the name, didn't she?"

"Yeah, but she's usually frustrated when she says it."

"It was her gift of love at your birth. A name is the first and greatest gift we give one another."

"I never thought of it like that."

"What else would a name be?" the guru says.

"A curse."

Like the Zuckerman name. Like growing up as the grandchild of a survivor and everything you do is supposed to prove that God had a reason for allowing the Zuckerman line to survive. But what if God had nothing to do with it? What if it was just luck? Or fate?

Or nothing at all. What if it happened just because?

"I don't want to talk about this," I say. "I want to talk about you taking my mother away."

"You're wrong about that," he says.

"You're not going to India together?"

"We are going on a journey. That's true. What's not true is that I'm taking her. She's choosing to go."

"She has children."

"I realize this."

"But you have no problem letting her abandon us."

"I don't understand. You have a father, don't you?"

"More or less."

"So you are not abandoned."

"We're abandoned by her. Not by him."

"I see. It *feels* like abandonment to you," he says.

"What would it feel like if your mother left you when you were a kid?"

"My mother died at an early age."

"Oh."

I sit down on the mat in front of the guru. "So you lived with your father?" I say.

He shakes his head.

"I did not know him, Sanskrit."

"Who raised you?"

"I was taken in by—I think you call it an orphanage."

"I didn't know that. I'm sorry."

"It's nothing to be sorry about. These are the cards—What's the expression?"

"The cards you were dealt."

"Yes," the guru says.

"They're bad cards."

"I don't believe in bad or good cards."

"You're not Jewish. We've had a lot of bad cards in our history."

"My people have suffered as well. All people suffer. This is the first noble truth."

"Why make it worse by taking our mother?"

The guru takes a long breath and pulls his ankles in tighter. I cross my legs like him.

"Your mother and I have something special together. A bond that goes back in time."

"By time you mean February?"

"I mean a previous life."

"Oh, please," I say.

"You may not believe in such things, but I do."

"I think you've confused her. Maybe even brain-washed her."

"Your mother is making a choice. Just as you can make a choice."

"What is my choice?" I say.

"To come with us."

"To India?"

I laugh.

I wait for him to tell me it's a joke, but he doesn't. He slowly uncrosses his legs and recrosses them in opposite order, looking at me calmly the whole time.

"I'm inviting you," the guru says, "now that I see you could benefit from it."

"That's crazy," I say.

"Is it?"

"How could I benefit from going to India?"

"You are a spiritual seeker."

"I'm not a spiritual seeker. I'm a—whatever you call the opposite of that. I don't believe in anything. I'm supposed to, but I don't."

The faint sound of a gong chimes far down the hall. A yoga class is beginning in the big studio.

"Maybe I shouldn't have said that."

How dare I not believe when Zadie survived the

camps? When I owe my whole existence to that fact? I wait for something terrible to happen, for an artery to explode in my head or an earthquake to shake the ground out from under me.

Nothing happens, just a second gong tone from down the hall.

"I'm supposed to believe," I say. "I was born Jewish. I go to Jewish school. My grandfather—he left money so I'd be Jewish."

"You cannot pay someone to be as you wish them to be."

"That's what I told my parents. But it was his final gift."

"A gift that has become a burden."

I never thought of it like that. A gift from Zadie's perspective could be a burden from mine. God's gift to Zadie was a burden, too. God gave him his life, and Zadie was obsessed with being a success, like he had to prove he was worthy of it.

"Maybe it's time to lay down the burden," the guru says.

He says it like it's simple, but how do you do it? What does it even mean? Do I leave school? Do I stop being Jewish?

"You're asking many questions in your head," the guru says.

"Maybe."

"May I make a suggestion?"

I nod.

"Don't try to answer these questions," the guru says. "Let them remain questions for the time being."

"How can I not answer them?" I say.

"Because it's enough just to ask them," he says.

"But why ask if you're not going to look for an answer?"

"I'm open to an answer if it comes, but I'm not actively looking for one. It's a different way of approaching it. I don't try to figure it out. I simply get comfortable holding the questions."

I ask a question in my head:

Why is my mom so screwed up?

I try to do what the guru said and not answer it, but it's impossible. My head fills with reasons.

"Sanskrit."

The guru says my name. It snaps me out of it.

"You have to practice this technique," he says. "Don't expect to get it immediately."

I look across at him. We're both sitting far apart on the floor, but it feels like we're closer, like I could reach out and touch him.

"Come to India with your mother and I."

"What would I do in India?"

"Grow."

"I can grow here."

"True," the guru says. "But in India you might grow in a new way."

"What about school?"

"We have many schools in India. It would be your choice which one to attend."

"I wouldn't have Zadie's tuition money. Once I leave Jewish school, the money goes away. No second chances."

"You wouldn't need it there. We could get you into a private school that is affordable."

I stand up.

"I don't know what to say, guru."

"Don't say anything. Sit with the idea for a while. But it has to be your own choice. I would never tell you to leave school. Or your religion, for that matter. Sometimes, we return to the religion of our birth and find solace there. Other times, we must find the strength to rebel against it. Every journey is different."

"I don't know what my journey is," I say.

"How could you?" he says. "You're in the middle of it."

"You have no idea where you're going, do you?"

That's what the woman in Starbucks says.

They've renovated since I was here last, and I was in the pickup line instead of the ordering line.

"Sorry," I say, and I slip in behind her.

She grunts and turns her back to me. She stretches a little, then bends over to tie her sneaker. She's wearing black yoga pants with blue stripes on the thighs that come to a V in her private place. It reminds me of lights on a runway. I hate her, but I wish I were a pilot at the same time.

"Wait. I recognize you," the woman says.

She spins around, catching me looking at her butt. I quickly look up.

"The Center. Your mom is a teacher, right? I'm Sally."

"Hey, Sally," I say. She's the Asian woman who was ready to attack the guru with a yoga mat last week.

"Your mom is the luckiest woman in the world."

"She is?"

"If I had a guru interested in me? Wow. That's like dating God."

"He's not a god," I say. "He's just like you and me."

"Who says?"

"He says."

"Of course he does. If he was God, he wouldn't go around saying he was God. Only crazy people do that."

"Can I help the next guest," the barista says.

"Your mom is starting a whole new life," Sally says. "It's so exciting."

She goes to the counter, and the entire line moves up one step.

Mom's new life. Or *our* new life.

It's up to me. At least according to the guru.

I think about leaving Jewish school. Going in for my last day. Saying good-bye to everyone. The CORE boys would walk by, and I'd say, "Hey, I won't be around for Passover this year. I'm going to India."

They wouldn't believe it.

"Next guest," the barista says.

I usually order a mocha latte if Mom isn't around, a decaf organic soy fair trade latte if she's watching. She hates that I like coffee, but I can drink it in front of her as long as I transform it into something politically correct that tastes bad.

"What can we get you today?" the barista says. She's got on a starchy Starbucks apron and a hat adorned with multiple pins.

I say, "Do you have anything Indian?"

"You mean Native American. We don't say Indian anymore."

"We do if we mean something from India."

"Oh. Well, that's okay to say. But I don't think we have coffee from India."

"Do you have anything?"

"You mean like chai?"

"Right. That's what I mean."

"Grande chai latte," the barista says, writing it on the side of a cup. "And what's your name?"

"Sanskrit."

"Say again."

"Sanskrit. Like the language."

"Oh," she says. "No wonder you ordered the chai."

She passes my cup down to the coffee prep area, and I follow it.

"Grande chai latte for . . . Sanskrit," a barista calls. Then he chuckles.

"Good one, dude," he says, and passes me the drink. He's got a long beard braided with a red ribbon at the bottom.

"Do I need to do anything to it?" I say.

"Like what? Buy it a birthday gift?"

"No, like put sugar in it."

"It's already sweet."

"I've never had one before."

"Drink it, dude. Live a little."

I sit down at a table by the window. I take a sip of the chai. It's spicy, creamy, and sweet at the same time.

I take another sip.

I look out the window at traffic moving down San Vicente. I imagine I'm in a café in India watching traffic on a street in Mumbai.

I try to wrap my head around the idea. Mom, me, and the guru in India together.

A text chimes on my phone. It's Sweet Caroline.

wht hpnd w/ guru?

A wave of guilt hits me. How can I even think of leaving Sweet Caroline here alone?

But then I remember she hates spicy food. She hates most food, except chocolate. She also hates being dirty. I don't know much about India, but I know there's lots of spices and dirt. That would be like two strikes for her.

I decide that Sweet Caroline would be miserable in India, but she wouldn't be miserable here. It's true that Dad is irresponsible, but one extra person at his place wouldn't be so bad. Dad would take her to See's Candies and call her Sweet McGeet a hundred times a day.

She might even be happier.

I text her back:

tell u later

Because I need some time to think this over.

Just then, Talya Stein and Melissa Rabinowitz sit down outside the window. They're both friends of The Initials. Their table is maybe twelve inches from mine, only on the other side of the glass. I'm trying to ignore them, but they're too close. Melissa does that thing where she takes her long skirt and tucks it between her legs so it's out of the way. She's wearing tights underneath with a speckled pattern, colored dots traveling up and down her legs. I peek through the window a few times. For some reason, they haven't noticed me. Or maybe they have, and they just don't care.

I go back to my chai, then a shadow passes across the window. The Initials sits down.

Judi. She's not The Initials anymore. Just Judi.

She's in the seat right next to mine on the other side of the window. If we were at the same table, we'd be sitting next to each other.

I glance at her, but she doesn't see me. It's like I'm invisible, even though there's only a pane of glass between us.

I take a slug of chai. The spice hits my tongue, and it wakes me up. It was the old Sanskrit who looks at girls through windows and does nothing. What about this Sanskrit? The one who calls The Initials by her real name?

This Sanskrit knocks on the window.

That's what I do now. I tap. The girls are startled. They peer into the window. It's sunny out, so the reflection must make it hard to see inside. It occurs to me that they weren't ignoring me. They really couldn't see me.

Judi presses her face to the window and cups her hands around her eyes like she's looking through binoculars.

"Sanskrit!" she says through the glass.

She says something to the girls, then hops up from her seat, takes her backpack and coffee, and comes into Starbucks.

"I can't believe it's you," she says.

"I can't believe it's me either," I say.

Judi laughs. I made Judi laugh!

"I need to talk to you," she says.

"I need to talk to you, too," I say.

She doesn't laugh that time. Bummer. For a second I thought I was going to repeat everything she said, and she would love it. Now I see it's going to be more complicated than that.

"This is perfect timing," Judi says. "I mean, if you're not in the middle of something."

"I'm not. Well, I am. But I'm just thinking about stuff."

"What kind of stuff?"

"Long story."

"Can I ask you about your mother?"

"My mother?" I say, a little disappointed.

"If it's not too painful," Judi says. "I just need a little background. So we can write an introduction and everything."

Judi puts a hand on my forearm.

"Of course," I say. I'm hoping she'll keep her hand on my arm, or even move it up to my shoulders, but she doesn't. She sits across from me and takes a pad out of her backpack. She taps a quick text into her phone, then puts it into her bag and directs all her focus towards me.

"Tell me about her," Judi says.

"What do you want to know?"

"Tell me what she likes."

"She likes yoga. And tofu. And music with chanting."

"I thought you were Jewish."

"We are. But you can be Jewish and do yoga."

"Right, but the chanting? What's that?"

"It's nondenominational chanting."

"Are you sure it isn't Buddhism or something like that?"

"Mom doesn't belong to any particular religion. She dabbles."

"Okay, let's change the subject," Judi says. She

clicks the pen and scribbles on her pad. "I'm going to say that your mom has a lot of interesting hobbies and she likes to exercise."

"That's true," I say.

"Does she have any cool expressions? Like, if she was a sports team, what would her motto be?"

"Eat healthy."

"That's not really a motto."

Eat healthy so you can poop well. That's Mom's real motto. But I'm not telling Judi.

I say, "I just remembered Mom's favorite expression: *Whoever saves one life, saves the entire world.*"

Mom doesn't even know that expression, but I remember it from a B-Jew screening of *Schindler's List* this year.

"That's a beautiful one," Judi says. "From the Talmud."

Judi writes a few things, then puts the pad down.

"This is just so weird talking to you," she says.

"I'm weird?"

"I mean like weirdly familiar."

"How can it be familiar? We haven't talked since second grade."

"So you do remember!" she says.

"Sort of. It's a blur."

She crosses her legs under her long skirt.

"Maybe it's not the time," she says.

"We're here, aren't we?"

"We're here," she says. She looks out the window.

Talya and Melissa are gone. We're alone.

Not alone. Together.

We're together again. I dreamed about this so many times over the years, but now that it's happening, it feels fake.

"To be honest, second grade was a tough time for me," Judi says.

"You didn't seem like you were having a tough time," I say.

"I was only seven. How can anything be tough at seven, right?"

I think about my second grade. Tough.

"No, I get it," I say. "But what was tough about it for you?"

"We had that mean teacher. What was her name?"

"Ms. Shine."

"Right. She was so intense. She gave us, like, two hours of homework, even though we were supposed to have thirty minutes. I got a migraine my first day of second grade," Judi says.

"I didn't know that."

"It was from stress. I used to get them when I was younger."

"Not now?"

"They're rare now. Maybe I grew out of them. I hope so."

"But back then you had them."

"Yeah, I think I was scared my first day. I would have left the class, but you were so nice to me."

"Me? What did I do?"

"It really is a blur for you, huh? Do you remember you sharpened my pencil?"

"I would never sharpen a girl's pencil."

"Now you wouldn't."

"What does that mean?"

"I don't know. You kind of—do your own thing."

"Maybe I'm shy."

"You don't seem shy this moment."

I smile and she smiles back.

"So tell me about the first day of second grade," I say.

"Okay. I broke a pencil, and I was about to get up when you reached over and asked me if you could sharpen it for me."

"No way."

"Then you took my whole pencil case up to the electric sharpener."

"That's so embarrassing."

"You took them out one by one, and you were just sawing away at the things for, like, ten minutes. Ms. Shine finally said, 'Are you going to be a lumberjack, Mr. Zuckerman?' and everyone laughed."

I'm watching her as she tells the story, and even though I don't remember it exactly, something about it sounds right, like a picture slowly coming into focus.

"The whole class laughed at me? Great, I looked like a jerk on my first day."

"I didn't laugh, Sanskrit. I was grateful that you helped me." Judi pulls her backpack onto her lap and hugs it to her. "I remember that day really well," she says, "because it was the only thing that made me want to come back to school the next day."

I take a sip from my cup and the taste of India fills my mouth.

India. I was actually considering the idea a few minutes ago. But everything feels different now that Judi and I are talking. Now that there's a chance for us.

"I remember something about second grade," I say.

"What?"

"Valentine's week."

I'm about to tell her it was the greatest week of my life, when I see her face has gone pale. She bites at her thumbnail.

"What's wrong?" I say.

Before she can answer, Barry Goldwasser walks up.

"I turn my back for one minute," he says, "and Zuckerman slides in like a snake in the garden."

"You're crazy," Judi says.

"How is my beauty?" he says to Judi. He looks around the room. "Have the *frummers* left the building?"

"All clear," she says.

I'm wondreing why he would care if any religious

people are around when he leans over and kisses her.

Barry claps me on the shoulder like nothing just happened. His voice turns serious. "How are you doing, buddy? For real."

I can't speak.

"Judi's been giving you the third degree, huh?" he says. "I know, she sent me a text."

He pulls up a chair, straddles it backwards, and leans towards me, his arms crossed along the back edge.

I'm stunned. I can't stop thinking about the kiss.

I say, "Are you two—"

"Together?" Barry says. He smiles.

"We keep it low key," Judi says. "You understand."

"Of course."

"Back to business," Barry says.

"I don't want you to worry about this event," he says. "We're taking care of everything. God willing, your mother will be restored to health and back to you soon."

"God willing," I say.

"In the meantime, we do what we can."

He takes the pad out of Judi's hands and starts to read.

"Interesting. Who's doing the intro?" he says.

"It's up to Sanskrit."

"What's up to me?"

"The dean is going to make a speech," Judi says, "but one of us should introduce you. To show that the students are behind you."

"Happy to do it," Barry says. "In fact, I'd be honored."

"You kind of always do it," Judi says.

"Sorry if I'm the president and I have responsibilities," Barry says.

"I don't want to get into this again," she says.

"That's convenient," Barry says. He looks at me and rolls his eyes like we're in on it together. Boys vs. girls. It's the same thing Dad does when he's arguing with Mom.

"Do we have to fight in front of Sanskrit?" Judi says. "He's got enough on his mind."

Barry backs down.

"You are so right," he says. "Apologies all around. I don't know what I was thinking. Let me be a mensch here. It's up to you, Sanskrit. Whoever you're comfortable with."

I want to hurt Judi by choosing Barry. I want to hurt Barry by choosing Judi. I want to hurt both of them by canceling the whole event.

Or I could just tell the truth. Do it right now, fast, like dropping a guillotine.

I imagine their faces when I tell them I made the whole thing up.

Barry has his hand on Judi's back. He's stroking her

slowly as the two of them wait for me to make a decision about who should give the speech.

I look from Barry to Judi.

Not Judi anymore. Not my Judi. Someone else's.

The Initials. I want to call her The Initials again. It
was a mistake to switch back to her name.

"I want her to do the introduction," I say.

The Initials looks happy. I'm expecting Barry to be
upset, but he goes into Barry mode, giving my shoulder
a friendly clench.

"Good choice," he says. "This event is going to be so
special. I'm very happy about all of this."

"Me, too," I say. "I'm happy, too."

"I'm miserable."

That's what I tell Crystal when she asks me how I'm doing.

She leans across the reception desk at the Center and says, "I'm sorry to hear that. Do you want to talk about it?"

I almost tell her everything. How the guru invited me to go to India, how it seemed like a crazy idea. But that was before. Before I knew Judi had a boyfriend.

Now leaving the country seems like a great idea.

I'm not saying I'm going, but I really want to talk to the guru about it.

My phone chimes. Another text from Sweet Caroline:

wht hpnd!?!

I ignore it.

"I need to talk to the guru," I tell Crystal.

"He's in private session," Crystal says. "He can't be interrupted."

"This is important."

"If you can wait an hour—"

"Where is my mom?"

"She's not here."

"When will she be back?"

Crystal looks at the schedule.

"She has class at seven a.m. tomorrow."

My head is spinning. I think about going home and waiting for Mom, but I can't talk to her about this. I need to talk to the guru. I have to ask him about India, if he was serious about it.

"I just remembered. I have to get something from my mom's locker," I say.

"Do you know the combination?" Crystal says.

"Of course. She gave it to me."

Goal weight. Actual weight. Goal weight.

That way she never forgets.

I rush down the hall.

"Take your shoes off!" Crystal calls after me.

I peek through the window of the big studio, but there's a class in there, a sea of tanned flesh and muscled butts.

I check the smaller studio. There's a class in there, as well. Women with their backs arched over giant yoga balls.

I remember there's a private room in the back behind

the office. Sometimes Mom goes in there to meditate before her class.

I walk towards the office, glancing over my shoulder to make sure nobody is watching me.

There's a handwritten sign on the door of the private room:

DO NOT ENTER.
PRIVATE SESSION IN PROGRESS.

I ignore the sign, and I open the door.

The guru isn't there.

Instead I find Sally meditating in the middle of the room with her eyes closed. She's wearing a giant skirt, fabric spilling onto the floor around her.

"Ohhh—"

Sally moans loudly, and her head swings from side to side.

I start to back out the door, when something under her skirt moves. It takes a moment to understand what I'm seeing. There are two colors, the white of the skirt around Sally's waist, and the blue of the fabric peeking out beneath it—

The blue fabric moves, and Sally moans again.

"I'm looking for the guru," I say.

"What?!" she says, and her eyes pop open.

She jumps up, and I see a flash of her bare legs, then two other legs as the yards of blue fabric pull away from her. A head pops out as if being born from between her legs.

The guru's head.

He blinks as his eyes adjust to the light in the room.

Then he sees me.

"Sanskrit," the guru says.

I turn and run.

Ohhhh—

I can still hear Sally moan in my mind.

I race past the stinky yoga women's shoes and out the front door of the Center. I'm ready to run home, but my stomach clenches and I think I'm going to throw up, so I turn into the alley between the Center and Le Pain Quotidien restaurant.

I double over with my hands on my knees, trying to breathe, trying not to throw up. I smell baking bread from the restaurant, and it makes me gag.

"Sanskrit, why did you run?"

I turn to find the guru standing at the head of the alley. He looks at me innocently, as if he's confused by my reaction.

"That was disgusting," I say.

"Not disgusting," he says. "But unfortunate. It was not meant for your eyes."

"Don't talk to me like I'm a child."

"You're not a child. I know this," he says.

"The least you could do is lie, tell me it wasn't what I thought it was."

"I don't lie," the guru says. "But it might not have been what you thought it was."

"I thought you were in love with my mother. Why would you do that with someone else?"

"I do love your mother."

"So she knows about this?"

"She knows I love people."

"Mother Teresa loved people, too. She didn't have sex with them."

"You're right."

"So Mom doesn't know," I say. "Yet."

The guru holds up his hands, trying to calm me. But I won't have it.

"You said we could go to India! We would start a new life together."

"We can," the guru says. "The invitation stands. Is that why you've come? To tell me what you decided?"

He smiles. He steps towards me.

"What have you decided, Sanskrit?"

"I've decided you can go to hell," I say.

"How do you know
you can trust the guru?"

That's what I ask Mom when I get home. I want to tell her what I've seen, just blurt it out the minute I get into the kitchen, where she's arranging arugula leaves on a plate, but I think that would be a mistake. Mom might accuse me of lying to her, making things up to ruin her life.

"How can I trust him?" Mom says.

She holds out an arugula leaf for me to take a bite.

"I'm not hungry," I say.

"Please try it," Mom says.

I open my mouth and let her put it in.

"How does it taste?" she says.

"It's spicy."

"How did you know it was okay to eat?" Mom says.

"That's a weird question."

"How do you know it wasn't poisoned, for instance?"

"You're freaking me out, Mom."

"How do you know?"

"Because you gave it to me. You're my mother."

"Mothers go crazy. You see it on the news sometimes, how they drive into a lake with their kids in the car."

"Remind me never to drive with you again."

"I'm just saying you ate it because you trust me. You know me, and you trust me. It's as simple as that, right?"

"Maybe."

Mom smiles, puts more arugula on the plate. "That's how I feel about the guru."

"What if he did something to make you feel differently?"

"Like what?"

"Like something."

Mom looks concerned.

"What are you telling me?" she says.

I try to find the words, but I can't.

"Nothing," I say.

Mom puts down the tray and comes over.

"You're worried about me," she says. "I think that's sweet."

She hugs me tight.

"What are you doing?" I say.

"I'm hugging my son," she says, like it's something she does all the time.

It doesn't stop at the hug. She keeps her arms around me, pulling me close to her. She plants a kiss in my hair.

"Cut it out," I say, and I twist away from her.

"You're too old for a hug?"

"Not too old," I say. "It's just weird."

Mom rolls her eyes at me, then goes back to her salad.

I watch her moving lettuce around on the tray, cutting cubes of baked tofu to lay around the perimeter. She hums softly to herself as she does it.

Softly.

Ever since Mom met the guru, her energy has changed.

She's softer now, more open.

She sings to herself. She dances around the house. She's nice to me.

That's when it hits me: Mom's happy.

If I tell her what I saw at the yoga studio, she's going to hate me. That's if she even believes me.

I consider not saying anything. I could leave Mom alone, let this all happen like it's going to happen. If God is really in charge like Herschel says, then I can let him take care of it, can't I?

But what if he's not in charge and I let my mother go to India with a guy who is cheating on her?

I can't tell her, but maybe I can show her.

A plan is coming together, a way I might be able to get my mother back. But I'm going to need Sweet Caroline's help.

"We've got a surprise for you, Mom."

I'm listening in on the phone as Sweet Caroline talks to Mom.

"What kind of a surprise?" Mom says.

"If I tell you, it's not a surprise!"

Sweet Caroline doesn't know what the real surprise is, but this is part of the plan we worked out last night. I took her aside for a sibling meeting and broke the news to her. I didn't tell her about the guru sleeping around, only that he wasn't giving up on Mom.

"You said you'd get him to leave Mom alone," she said.

"He was going to, but he changed his mind," I said.

"But he promised."

"People don't always keep their promises," I told her.

"Tell me something I don't know," Sweet Caroline said.

She said it like some tough kid in a movie about

runaways, and I almost hugged her. Which of course would have been a mistake.

"I've got another idea," I said.

"Tell me what I should do," Sweet Caroline said. And I laid out the plan. At least her part of it.

That's what got me to this place. It's early afternoon, and I'm on a street south of Olympic, close to Santa Monica College. It's not a bad neighborhood, but it's nothing like Brentwood. Small houses, some of them with bars over the windows. That's how you know the quality of the neighborhood in Los Angeles. Check the first-floor windows.

"We'll be there in ten minutes," Sweet Caroline says over the phone. "Mom's getting her keys."

"There's a church on the corner. Meet me in front," I say, and I hang up.

The plan.

I knew the guru would be careful after I walked in on him at the Center, and I was right. I followed him to this neighborhood yesterday.

He's here again today.

I start to have second thoughts. But Mom and Sweet Caroline are already on their way. It's too late for second thoughts.

I sit on a bench in front of the church and wait for them.

There's a statue of a saint looking out over the garden.

God is everywhere. That's what Rabbi Silberstein says.

Maybe it's true, and maybe it's the problem. God has so much territory to cover that he can't focus on any particular thing.

I look to the saint in the garden for guidance, but he's got nothing for me. He's staring straight ahead, lost in thought. A bird lands on his head, flapping its wings twice before taking off again.

Mom's Volvo pulls into the parking lot. I motion for her to pull into an empty space.

"What are we doing in a church?" Mom says when she gets out.

"We're not going to church. We're going to someone's house down the street."

"What are you up to, Sanskrit?"

"It's a surprise," I say.

"I told you, Mom," Sweet Caroline says.

Sweet Caroline gets out of the wagon. She smiles, excited about it all.

"Down the street," I say. "Follow me, everyone."

Mom holds Sweet Caroline's hand, then reaches over to take mine, but I pull it away. The new, happy Mom does crazy things like trying to hold her kids' hands in public.

"It's the little green house over here," I say.

"Whose house is this?" Mom says.

"Mom, just let us surprise you," Sweet Caroline says.

We walk down the driveway. I'm thinking we could ring the front door and see what happens, but I've already checked and I know the gate to the backyard is open.

"We have to go around to the patio," I say.

"Does my hair look okay?" Mom says.

I give her a look.

"Just in case," she says.

I open the gate silently, make Mom walk in ahead of me. Then I step in front of Sweet Caroline.

"Let me go first," I whisper.

"I want to see," she says.

"Please," I say. I'm trying to protect her, but she's not making it easy.

She slumps her shoulders and lets me go in front of her.

I guide Mom up the three steps onto the back patio behind the house.

"It's in there," I say, pointing to the big picture window and the screen door leading into the house.

The sound of laughter spills out from inside the house.

Mom's face goes pale.

I glance through the window.

The guru is in there. So is Sally. This is her house.

She's sitting on his lap, kissing him.

Mom doesn't move. She stares into the house, not saying a word.

She turns back to me.

"You did this," she says.

"What happening?" Sweet Caroline says. She's trying to come up on the patio, but I'm blocking the steps.

"You set me up," Mom says.

"No," I say. "I just wanted you to see the truth."

"What's going on, Mom?" Sweet Caroline says.

"Stay there!" Mom says, holding up a hand to stop Sweet Caroline from coming onto the porch. Mom's face is bright red.

"What did you do?!" Sweet Caroline says to me. "You made things worse!"

Mom points her finger at me.

"You did this," Mom says. "I don't know why, but you did it and I'll never forgive you."

"I'm sorry!" I say.

But why am I apologizing? I'm not the one cheating on Mom.

Mom pauses for a moment, caught between opening the door to the house and something else. What else?

She jumps from the porch, grabs Sweet Caroline, and rushes away, pulling Sweet Caroline the whole way.

I stand on the patio not knowing what to do. I look inside again. The guru is kissing Sally. Suddenly, he turns and looks at me. He rubs his eyes for a moment like he can't believe what he's seeing.

"Sanskrit?" His lips form the words.

He shifts Sally off his lap. He gets up and walks towards me.

I take off.

I hear the door open behind me.

"Stop, Sanskrit!" the guru shouts after me.

But I don't stop. I run.

"Mom is upside down, and it's all your fault."

Sweet Caroline confronts me on the front stoop to the house. She must have been watching through the front window, waiting for me to come home.

"Did you hear me? It's your fault," she says.

"Leave me alone," I say.

After I saw the guru, I ran until I couldn't breathe, until my sides were splitting, until I didn't recognize the neighborhood anymore.

Then I drifted through Santa Monica for a few hours, thinking about things. I considered going to Dad's, but how could he help?

"What was in that house?" Sweet Caroline says. "Mom wouldn't tell me."

"You're too young," I say.

"I'm not too young!"

"Fine," I say. "It was the guru. With another woman."

"Oh."

That's all she says.

"Now you know why Mom didn't tell you."

"Why would you bring Mom there?"

"I'm trying to save our family," I say.

"So you lied to me?"

"I didn't lie. I told you we'd get Mom back."

"We didn't," she says.

"What do you mean?"

"You have to get dressed. We're going to the Center."

"I'm not going."

"Yes, you are. It's Mom's good-bye party."

"Why would I go? Why would she go after what she's seen?"

"She's going, Sanskrit. That's all I know. She hasn't said a word since we came home except that I should get ready to go. And if I'm going, you're going."

Sweet Caroline is right. How can I let her go there alone with Mom, not knowing what Mom is going to do?

I walk into the living room, and sure enough, Mom is upside down. She's wearing her best skirt, a wide, loose, flowered fabric that is flopped down to cover her face and body while her bare legs stick up in the air. She looks like a wilted flower.

She doesn't speak to me.

I go to my room and change into my best pants and a button-down. I only have two button-downs, so it's not like there's a lot to choose from.

A couple minutes later, Sweet Caroline knocks on my door, and I follow her down the hall. Neither of us says a word.

We go to the garage, and Mom is already in the car waiting.

I usually sit in the front, but I decide it's better to sit in the back today. I open the door and slide in next to Sweet Caroline.

Mom starts the car.

The garage door isn't open yet, and for a second, I think Mom might have gone crazy like she talked about the other day. She's going to keep the car running in a closed garage until we all die from carbon monoxide poisoning. I wonder how the *Jewish Journal* will massage that headline.

Mom revs the engine, glances in the rearview, realizes her mistake, and clicks the garage door opener.

The door creaks and rises in short jerks, a few inches at a time.

I'm thinking that Mom hates me right now, but she'll get over it. She's not really angry at me. She's angry at the guru. She's angry at the truth. She needs some time and then she'll understand.

It's better to have her in Los Angeles hating me than gone forever with the guru.

That's what I tell myself, anyway.

"Celebrate love!"

That's what Crystal shouts as we walk in, and a whoop goes through the crowd. There are nearly a hundred guests in the big yoga studio, spilling into the hallways, scattered throughout the Center. I recognize various yoga students, teachers, even the owners of the studio, who wear strange tunics everywhere they go. They're the ones who gave Mom the job in the first place.

A murmur goes through the crowd as people recognize Mom. They surround her and congratulate her. Mom is silent the whole time.

Mom scans the crowd, ignoring the people who are greeting her. She keeps moving until she finds the guru.

They stare at each other.

The crowd senses this and quiets down. People smile and step out of the way so they can get to one another.

The guru comes forward.

Mom does not.

She stays where she is, her eyes locked on him. The guru glances at me, then back at Mom.

"You broke my heart," Mom says.

There's a gasp in the room.

"I saw you," Mom says. "At Sally's house."

Sally stands there shocked. People look at her.

The guru clears his throat. "I was there. Yes."

"It wasn't the first time, was it?" Mom says.

"No," he says.

Mom starts to cry.

People in the room look at the ground.

"But you told me you loved me," Mom says through sniffles.

"I do," the guru says.

"You have an interesting way of showing it."

"Do we need to do this now?" the guru says. He motions to the people in the room.

"What better time?" Mom says. "Let's get it out in the open."

In a strange way, I'm proud of her. She's confronting him in front of everyone. Maybe I was wrong about Mom. Maybe she knows what she's doing more than I think she does.

"Very well," the guru says with a sigh. "You're asking if I love you, and I do. We are bonded together through time. You are my special flower."

"But you want a bouquet," Mom says.

"It's one of the ways we communicate love in our community. I share my physical self with my followers. I'm sorry if I misled you."

"What if I want to share myself with other men?"

"I would understand that."

"Oh my God," Mom says. She squeezes her head between her hands. "This is not—this is not the kind of relationship I want."

The guru comes closer to my mother.

"This doesn't change what you and I have," he says.

He reaches for her, but she twists away.

"No," Mom says.

"Please, Rebekah—"

"I won't do it. Not like this. I've had too many terrible relationships like this," Mom says, and she starts crying again.

I'm suddenly hopeful. Mom is breaking up with the guru. She's going to finish this once and for all, then she'll grab Sweet Caroline and me and bring us home.

She'll be heartbroken. But we'll be a family again. At least the assemblance of one.

"I can share you in many ways," Mom says to the guru. "But not like this."

"I see," the guru says. "You have—different customs here. This can be discussed."

"It can?" Mom says, softening.

"No, Mom!" I shout.

"Stay out of this, Sanskrit," she says.

Sweet Caroline grabs my arm.

"You should have told me," Mom says to the guru. "I shouldn't have had to find out from my son."

He bows his head in front of Mom.

She takes a step towards him.

He says something to her, so quietly that I can't hear it.

She's inches from him now, her face by his face, the two of them whispering to each other.

I want to scream again, run to Mom, and shake her until she wakes up.

But I can't move. I can only watch them drift towards each other slowly, so slowly, speaking the whole time, until at last their bodies are touching.

Then they reach out and wrap their arms around each other.

It reminds me of the moment they met, a fierce embrace that all but absorbs my mother into the guru's robes.

"A moment."

That's what the guru says on the staircase of the Center. I'm on my way out of the building when he appears at the top of the stairs.

"Sanskrit," he says. "Son."

"I'm not your son," I say.

"We're all God's children."

"You're not God."

He smiles.

"It is said that after the Buddha achieved enlightenment, he walked out into the world and nobody knew it had happened because he looked the same. They only knew later, from his actions and words."

"So you might be God? That's what you're saying?"

"No, I'm not God. No more so than any of us. But I was touched by God. That's how I became a guru."

The sound of a flute drifts down from the party.

"If you were touched by God, then tell me what he looks like."

"I didn't see him. I experienced him," the guru says. "Just like you did."

"What are you talking about?"

"You have not felt the presence of God?"

"Never," I say.

"Yet I can feel his presence in you."

"I don't want anything to do with God. Or gurus. Or religions. Or any of it."

"It's not too late for you to come with us," the guru says.

I push open the front door.

The guru says, "I know why you did what you did at Sally's house."

I stop halfway out the door.

"Maybe I would have done the same thing if I were in your place," he says.

"Why are you telling me this?"

"Because I forgive you."

"I don't need your forgiveness," I say.

"But I need to give it to you. For myself. Without forgiveness, how can we move forward?"

"I don't believe in you."

That's what I tell *HaShem* as I walk through Brentwood.

"I never really believed in you, but I was trying to give you a chance. Whoever you are. Whatever you are. I gave you a chance, but that's over."

I walk past the shops and restaurants on San Vicente. They're starting to fill up with the dinner crowd. I see people through the windows, laughing over plates of food.

I stop at a place where two streets merge together in a *V* shape. It's a mini park of trees and grass.

"I prayed to you when my parents were fighting and you didn't keep them together. I prayed for The Initials and you brought her back to me, only to give her a boyfriend. You stole my best friend from me in Israel. And now you're taking my mother."

I step into the park. I run my hand down the rough bark of a tree.

I imagine what I must look like. A crazy boy on San Vicente, shouting like a homeless man. Maybe this is what makes people homeless. They're not crazy on their own, but life has driven them crazy. A terrible God has stolen their lives, and they've snapped. Now they stand on street corners, in parks, in alleyways, on the beach in Santa Monica—and they shout at heaven.

Just like me.

It's almost funny, this idea. Because I realize I've found my group.

It's not the Jews or the Sikhs or the yoga devotees. It's not the good Jewish kids at my school or the followers of the guru.

I belong to the abandoned. We shout at the sky and the sky does not answer.

I haven't been touched by God. The guru was wrong about that. If there's a God at all, I've been stepped on by him. Zadie was stepped on, along with most of our family, in the Holocaust.

I sit at the base of the tree in the dark. My legs grow cold under me.

Eventually, the streetlights pop on along San Vicente Boulevard as twilight turns to evening.

A night bird calls from somewhere in the tree above me.

People laugh and clink glasses at the Italian restaurant across the street.

Life goes on, and God doesn't care. So why should I?

My phone vibrates in my pocket.

I stand up and take it out. It's a text message from Judi:

At school. Where r u!!!???

"How could you forget about it?"

The Initials meets me at the front door of school. She's frantic but beautiful in a long silky dress.

I say, "I've got a lot going on right now."

She backs off a bit.

"Of course you have. I'm sorry to yell at you, Sanskrit. Let's just get you in there."

She starts walking, and I hurry along next to her.

"I have to tell you something," I say.

"Could you tell me on the way?"

"Would you just stop for a second?"

She pauses, confused.

"What is it? Are you nervous about the event?"

"I'm in love with you," I say.

It pops out of me. Sometimes when you have nothing to lose, you do things you wouldn't imagine doing any other time.

"What did you just say?"

"I've always loved you. Ever since that spelling bee in second grade."

"I don't believe it."

"I know you have a boyfriend and you're, like—on a whole different social strata than me."

"That's not true," she says.

"I don't have any friends."

"What about The Rabbi?"

"Herschel? He used to be my friend. Not really now."

A cheer echoes from the gymnasium and bounces down the hall.

"They're all cheering for you," The Initials says. "What do you call that?"

"They're cheering because my mother got hit by a car."

"Good point," she says.

"Just forget it. Forget I said anything. I needed to get it off my chest. I'll bury it again, and we can go back to being acquaintances tomorrow."

"But I want to talk to you about it, Sanskrit."

"You do?"

"I want to ask you about second grade. Just not now."

Suddenly, I feel happy. More than happy. Hopeful. Maybe I've lost everything but gained back The Initials.

Wait. Not The Initials.

"Judi," I say.

"Yes?"

"Maybe we can go out after the fund-raiser and talk about everything?"

"After," she says. "Definitely."

"Why does God bring suffering upon us? What purpose does it serve?"

Rabbi Silberstein pauses, looking out at the audience in the gymnasium.

"We do not have an answer. We cannot know the mind of God. We only know that suffering is visited on some more than others. In this matter, the Zuckerman family has had more than their fair share. Theirs is a story of suffering . . . and survival."

He doesn't say it directly, but everyone knows he's talking about Zadie. It's not like I'm the only grandchild of a survivor in the school. There are a few of us, and everyone knows who we are.

"Now this family is going through another trial," he says. "And we as a community are called to action."

Applause spreads through the gymnasium. I look around and see that practically the whole school is here. The professors, the head of school, the dean, and all the students. Tyler stands in the front row with tears in his eyes, clapping his hands.

Everyone is here except Herschel. It looks like my old friend has boycotted my fund-raiser. He's the only one who knows the truth, so I can't say I'm surprised.

"We do not act out of goodness," Rabbi Silberstein says, "though we may indeed be good. We act because it is our duty. As we celebrate the Passover holiday this year and remember how God brought our people out of bondage in Egypt, we will remember, too, the debt we owe to him for this gift. It is our responsibility to act in the lives of others. We are the hands of *HaShem* in this world. This is the essence of *tzedakah*. You, the young people in our community, are practicing it today. And I'm proud of you."

Another long round of applause.

Judi waves her hand in the air, getting the dean's attention. He motions us over.

The dean steps up to the podium and says, "Thank you, Rabbi Silberstein, for that inspiring call to action. Speaking of calls, our annual building fund drive is coming up after Pesach, and your phones are going to ring—"

The students groan.

"I admit, it was a bad segue," the dean says. "But it's my job to remind you."

The students laugh.

"It's good to laugh at times like these," he says. "But now let's turn our attention to the serious matter at hand. It's time for me to introduce the real hero of the evening, Aaron Zuckerman."

Judi hooks her arm in mine and walks me to the microphone.

"I've had the opportunity to spend some time with Sanskrit over the last few days," she says to the crowd. She smiles at me. "To be honest, we hadn't spoken much in the last few years. It's strange how that happens. You can be so close to someone yet drift away from them. Childhood friends become strangers, best friends become acquaintances. We lose touch with each other, even when—when it may not be what we intended."

She looks me in the eye.

She says, "How sad that it took something like this to bring us back together."

My chest gets tight. This is what she wants to talk to me about after the event. Getting back together. She's giving me a preview in front of the whole school.

I look over at Barry Goldwasser, and I laugh to myself. Why was I so worried about him? He's nothing, insubstantial. I thought he was standing in the way, but it turns out he's not in the way at all.

Maybe that week in second grade wasn't the end of my love life but the beginning, like an appetizer that happened long before the meal. And now the rest of high school is going to be the meal of a lifetime.

Judi finishes and steps away from the microphone.

I hesitate.

I just have to get through this event, then Judi and I will be together. That's what I tell myself.

I step up to the podium.

"I am the grandson of a survivor," I say.

The crowd goes silent. I don't talk about this in school because I don't want people to ask me about it. It's one of those things that gives you instant credibility, but a lot of responsibility, too. You're not just Jewish. You are one of the miracles. Why did your family survive when so many did not? It's not enough that you're alive; you have to do something to prove that you're worth it.

It's a lot of pressure, and I don't want it. Not usually, at least.

But tonight I don't care. I tell everyone who I am, not because I'm proud of it or even because I'm humbled. I tell them because I want them to feel bad for me.

"My family has had many trials," I say. "But I'm no different than any of you. We all have trials. I don't know why God has chosen me for this test so young. It's hard to think of yourself as lucky in this sort of situation. But I have to look for the spiritual in it, in all things."

I'm so full of crap, I can't believe it. The rabbi is smiling and nodding, urging me on. I can see he's surprised, too. He probably thinks I've had some kind of conversion. I almost think so myself.

So I keep going.

I'm listening to myself speak, but I have no idea what I'm saying. I'm parroting Herschel, the Bible, Moses, some lecture I vaguely remember from Hebrew school when I was ten. It's a performance par excellence, and all during it, I'm waiting for *HaShem* to strike me down, send a lightning bolt, cut the power, do something to put an end to it. If there were a God, he would surely stop me.

But nothing happens.

I finish to rousing applause. The dean steps up and hugs me in front of the whole school. He waits for the crowd to quiet down, and then he says, "Could you tell us a little about your mom's condition? None of us have been able to see her, and it would help us to know."

He steps away from the podium, and I burst into tears.

The dean is shocked. He puts his arm around me, which just makes me cry harder.

I don't know why I'm crying. Maybe it's because I'm such a liar. Maybe it's because I'm really losing my mother, just not in the way people think, not in some noble and terrible way like a car accident, but in an embarrassing way via YouTube and yoga.

Maybe I'm crying because I have to figure out what I'm going to do next. Even as I stand up here in front of all these people, my mind is coming up with another plan to get me out of this.

A bigger plan. The exit strategy.

I'm going to wait until Mom goes to India, and then I'm going to lie again.

I'm going to say that she died.

It's terrible and yet it's perfect. Mom will be in India, so nobody will see her. Sweet Caroline and I will be staying with Dad, just like we would if it really happened. I can even say the funeral was held in Boston, where Mom was born.

It's a crazy idea, but no crazier than the ideas that got me here in the first place.

I wipe the tears from my eyes. I clear my throat. I lean into the microphone.

"My mother is not well," I say to the crowd. "The doctor says the prognosis is—" I choke on the sentence, clear my throat again. "The prognosis is very grave."

The entire gymnasium is silent, maybe five hundred people with their heads bowed.

Just then I hear a hinge squeak in the back of the gym. The double doors swing open, and Herschel walks in. He's in full Jewish regalia, the black suit and hat I've come to know so well.

He's not alone. There's a woman with him.

"This is Mrs. Zuckerman," Herschel announces to the room loudly. "Sanskrit's mother."

Heads turn, necks crane, all focus shifts to the double doors at the back of the room.

Mom stands there in her party dress, light from

the hallway streaming in around her. I can see Sweet Caroline a couple steps behind her in the hall.

"Sanskrit, what are you telling these people?" Mom says.

I look at her, then I look at the school, the five hundred or so people now staring at me.

"It's a miracle!" I say.

"I don't know who you are anymore."

Mom is calm as she says it, which just makes it worse. We're heading home from school after an hour-long interrogation in front of a group of administrators and prominent faculty members. I had no choice but to tell them the whole story of my lie. Needless to say, it did not go over well.

"I thought you were a good kid," Mom says.

"I was. I am."

She shakes her head like I'm wrong. I have to bite my lip to keep from saying more.

There's an accident on San Vicente, and traffic isn't moving. Mom beeps the horn and she's met with a chorus of answering beeps.

"You told everyone your mother was in an accident? That's like a wish. You put that energy out into the universe—what if it came true?"

I glance in the backseat. Sweet Caroline is quiet for one of the few times in her life.

"Don't look at your sister. She has nothing to do with this."

"She knew what was going on."

"That's your excuse?" Mom says. "You're going to blame a twelve-year-old?"

I shake my head *no*.

A siren blares as an ambulance slowly makes its way through traffic.

Cars attempt to get out of the way, but there's nowhere to go.

Mom slaps the wheel with an open palm. "You told them I was dying?"

"You're leaving," I say. "That's like dying."

"No it's not, Sanskrit. It's the opposite."

"Not to me."

I look to Sweet Caroline for some support, but she's got her headphones on. Her eyes are shut and her head is bopping to music.

I say, "I don't understand how you could still go with him after what happened."

"I don't expect you to understand," Mom says.

"Explain it to me. Explain how you could know about the guru—"

"It's not about the guru!" Mom says. "It's never really been about the guru."

I look at Mom, her fingers clenched white against the steering wheel.

"Then what's it about?" I say.

"It's about me," Mom says.

She beeps the horn hard, and the car in front of us puts a hand out the window and gives her the finger.

"When I imagined my life, I didn't imagine it like this," Mom says.

"Like what?"

"This, Sanskrit! This car. This job. This stupid community we live in. Going to parent-professor conferences and teaching yoga to spoiled housewives."

"Wow."

"I had dreams, Sanskrit. Bigger dreams."

"But you had a family," I say.

"I did. For your father's sake. And for your zadie."

I imagine the pressure on Mom to have kids. The children of survivors have to have kids. If not, the family line is wiped out. It's like spitting in God's face. That's what some people think.

"So you didn't want us?" I say.

"That's not true. I did it for other people, but I did it for myself, too. I wanted to be a mother."

"But you don't want to be *our* mother."

"I want to be your mother. I just—"

The ambulance whoops. It's a foot away, passing by my window. I see the driver's face frozen in concentration.

"I just want more," Mom says.

"More than us?"

Mom takes a long breath.

"Yes," she says.

The accident comes into view in front of us. A car is upside down on the median, surrounded by fire-fighters.

"What do you want, Sanskrit?"

The lights of the fire trucks turn Mom's face red, then dark, then red again.

I don't answer Mom's question, and she doesn't press me.

"Terrible accident," Mom says as she looks out the window. "I hope they'll be alright."

"I hope so, too," I say.

"A betrayal."

That's what the dean calls it at the review board meeting the next day. As it turns out, last night's stand and deliver was just the preliminaries. The formal hearing is today. Right now.

This would be the time for me to mount a defense. If only I had one.

The dean says, "You embarrassed the entire school, your family, and most of all, yourself."

He doesn't stop there. In fact, he's just getting started.

According to Jewish law, part of what makes meat kosher is the manner in which the animal is killed. It must die without experiencing pain or fear.

Evidently, I will not be kosher. Because my execution drags on for another hour.

When the dean finishes, each member of the review board takes a crack at me. Even Rabbi Silberstein is there, lecturing me on how many of God's mitzvahs I've broken. Dozens of them, according to the rabbi.

I don't doubt it.

When they've finished, I'm sent out of the room while they debate my fate.

I step out and Dorit, the Israeli office lady, won't even look at me.

"You can wait outside," she says, pointing to the door.

I step out of the office and sit on the bench in the hall.

Students pass by between classes. Nobody says a word to me. In one night I've gone from the most loved and pitied kid in school to the most shunned. I can't say I blame them.

I put my head down and wait.

"That was messed up on levels I can't even comprehend," Judi says. She's glaring down at me.

Last night she ran out of the gym when I tried to explain. Shouted and ran.

Now she looks down at me, her lips clenched, her hands on her hips

"You're a son of a bitch," she says.

"I know," I say.

"Worse than that. Worse than anything."

"You're right."

She starts to walk away. Then she comes back quickly.

"What really pisses me off is that you did it to me again," she says. "I let you do it."

"Do what?"

"Don't play dumb," she says.

"You said I did it again. I really don't know what you're talking about."

"Second grade, you jerk. You broke my heart."

"You're confused."

"I'm not confused. I know what happened," she says.

"Not that it matters now," I say, "but you broke up with me."

"That's what you think?"

"That's what I know. You stopped talking to me, and it destroyed me. I've spent the last eight years thinking about you."

"When did I break up with you?" she says.

"After Valentine's Day."

"Describe it to me."

I try to remember the exact moment, but it was so long ago. I've thought about it a million times, of course, but it's still fuzzy. I only know it became the defining week of my life.

"Let's hear it," Judi says.

"I don't remember every detail," I say.

"That's convenient, isn't it? Since you're the one who left me."

"That's not true."

"It's so true, you don't even know."

I try to think back to that time. Something is bothering me, some memory that I can't quite connect to.

"We were supposed to meet on the Tuesday after Valentine's Day," Judi says. "After school."

"I don't think so," I say.

"We planned it," Judi says. "Remember the slide?"

"Oh my God," I say.

I remember. The playground at Douglas Park. They had a new jungle gym with a slide set. There was a little secret room under the slide. Our favorite place to meet. We used to hold hands in there and talk about everything.

"We planned to have our first kiss that day," Judi says, "and you never showed up. I waited all afternoon for you, and you didn't come."

How is that possible? I was crazy about Judi. I would never stand her up, even in second grade.

What was I doing that day? I try to remember.

Mom was having a big fight with Dad. He'd forgotten Valentine's Day, and she spent the week freaking out. She needed someone to talk to. Even in second grade, I was that person. Her little man.

I wanted Mom to take me to meet Judi, but I couldn't ask her. She was going through too much. No matter how badly I wanted to be with Judi, I wouldn't leave Mom. She needed me. That's what I thought.

"You barely remember," Judi says. "It was just second grade, so what's the big deal, right? But it was a big deal to me. A very big deal."

"I remember now," I say.

"You do."

"Yes."

"It only took you, like, nine years."

"I'm sorry, Judi."

She studies my face, trying to see if I'm telling the truth.

"You stood me up for my first kiss, Sanskrit. Then you pretended you didn't know me in school the next day. That's not the kind of thing I can forgive."

"I was embarrassed," I say.

And I think my mind played some kind of trick on me. It told me Judi broke up with me so I wouldn't have to take responsibility. I spent years believing my own story.

"You said you loved me last night," Judi says. "That's why I was confused. But now I know that you lied."

"Not about that," I say.

"I see, so you only selectively lie? It doesn't work like that. You're a liar, Sanskrit. I can never trust you again. None of us can."

"You sound like Herschel."

The office door opens.

"Mr. Zuckerman," Dorit says. "They're ready for you."

"Time to throw myself on the mercy of the court," I say.

"You don't deserve mercy," Judi says, and she walks away.

She's right. I don't deserve it.

That's exactly what the review board says when I go back in. I don't deserve mercy, but they've decided to give it to me anyway.

They stop short of expelling me. They don't want to destroy my chances for college and with it my opportunity to redeem myself. Since there are only eight weeks left in junior year, they allow me to finish them from home.

And after that?

I'm not invited back.

"You got what you wanted."

"What did I want?" Herschel says.

"They threw me out of school," I say. "Only in slow motion."

He stands next to me as I sort through my cabinet. Books that belong to me in one box, books that belong to the school in another.

"I finish the year at home, take my exams early, then I'm out. B-Jew and Sanskrit are parting ways."

"I'm sorry," Herschel says.

"Why would you be sorry? It's what you wanted, right? That's why you brought Mom to the fund-raiser."

"I wanted to make things right."

"How do you know what's right?"

"I pray to know."

"I love that. I love how people do messed-up things in the world, and then they say it's God's will. Like you have a direct line into what's right and wrong."

It's between classes, and the halls are full of students.

"No," Herschel says. "She fell, too."

"For someone else."

"For me, Sanskrit. We fell for each other. It happens, you know. Not everyone lives in your universe of unrequited love. Love requites. At least it did with Chana."

"Chana." I repeat the name, enjoying the guttural *chet* sound, the Hebrew letter that you pronounce like you're clearing your throat. It makes her sound rough and sexual and Israeli all at the same time.

"We fell for each other, Sanskrit." He lowers his voice and leans towards me. "We even slept together."

"Newsflash: you're a virgin."

"No."

"How could you keep something like that a secret? That's the most important thing in the world."

"Not so important."

"What?! We've talked about sex for years. You never told me you knew how to do it."

"I don't know how to do it."

"You did it."

"I didn't know what I was doing. It just happened."

"Once?"

"A few times."

"Jesus Christ," I say.

Herschel winces. "The cursing—"

"What do you want from me? This is unbelievable news."

"It's not—You're not understanding me," Herschel says.

"I understand that you had sex," I say. "Though I admit I'm lacking certain critical details which you're more than welcome to describe to me."

"It's not what you think," he says.

"Well, what was it? What happened to the mysterious Chana?"

"She was from England. She went back home."

"Oh. That sucks."

"She had to."

"What am I missing?"

"She was with child."

"What?"

Herschel is speaking in biblical terms. But I know what he means. Pregnant.

"You have a kid?" I say.

"I don't."

"Wait. I'm confused. You said she was pregnant."

"We terminated the pregnancy."

"Oh my God."

"I took the life of a child," Herschel says.

His whole body changes. He leans against the wall, holding himself up with both arms.

"This is unbelievable," I say. "You didn't tell me any of this."

"It was a secret," he says.

He lets out a moan and slumps down to the

floor, sitting with his back against the wall.

I think of Herschel when he came back from Israel. He was different, but I thought it was because of the religious conversion. Formal words, formal dress, services every day . . .

I sit on the floor next to Herschel, up close so our shoulders are touching.

"I can't imagine how hard that must have been," I say. "But it's not like abortion is illegal in Israel. And it was your freshman summer. Nobody would blame you for not wanting to be a father."

"Why not a father?" Herschel says. "Who says I'm supposed to be free and doing whatever I want in the world? Nobody. Judaism does not say we are free. We are bound to God."

"You were a child. You didn't know."

"I was bar mitzvahed!" he says.

He means he was a man. He was responsible for his actions.

"You ask how I found God?" he says. "This is how. After it was done, my child came to me in a dream. Only he wasn't mine anymore. He was *HaShem's* child."

Herschel bites at his lip.

"I can never undo what I did, but I can spend my life making amends. I can cleave myself to his will. That's why I bought your mother to school. I was trying to do the right thing. I'm sorry if I caused you harm."

"You didn't do anything wrong." I say. "I got what I deserved."

He pats my forearm.

"God will find us, one way or the other," he says. "Some of us are stubborn, and the journey to him is hard. I pray it goes more easily for you than it did for me, my friend."

Herschel pulls himself up. He puts out a hand to help me up.

"Now you know everything," he says.

We hug briefly, and he pats me on the cheek.

I laugh a little. "You're like my zadie," I say.

"When is your mother leaving?"

"Tomorrow."

"Let me know if I can help in any way." He forces a half smile, then walks away down the hall.

"It's time."

It's Mom, calling to us from the living room.

Saturday morning. Moving day.

"Kids, I'm leaving," she says.

Sweet Caroline is crying in her bedroom. I hear the muffled sobs through the wall. Mom walks down the hall and goes into Sweet Caroline's room. I can't hear what they're saying exactly, but I can imagine it.

After a few minutes, Sweet Caroline's door opens, and Mom taps on my door.

"Sanskrit?"

I don't answer.

"I'm leaving now."

I hold my breath.

"Can I say good-bye?" Mom says.

She turns my doorknob, even though she's not allowed to come in without my permission. It's locked. I made sure of it.

"Please, Sanskrit."

My lungs are burning. I want to take a breath, inhale so hard that I pull Mom into the room.

"Your father is on his way over," Mom says. "Late as always. I have to leave or I'm going to miss my flight."

I press my face into the pillow and take a breath. My nose fills with the scent of lavender. That's the stuff Mom spritzes on the sheets when she gets them back from fluff-and-fold. Her little personal touch.

"I left a curry stew in the refrigerator," Mom says.

I don't acknowledge her.

"Sanskrit," Mom says, her face pressed close to my door. "I want to tell you—"

A taxi blows its horn in front of the house.

I want Mom to finish the sentence. What was she going to say?

I love you.

I'm sorry.

I don't want to go.

I'll never know.

I wait for the scraping at my door to stop. For Mom's footsteps to move away down the hall. For the front door to open and close. For the squeak of the cab's brakes as it pulls away on the street.

For the house to go quiet.

It does.

A few minutes later, there's a tap on my door.

I go over and pop the lock.

Sweet Caroline doesn't say anything. She just stands

there looking at the ground and chewing on a finger-nail.

I go back and lay on my bed, look up at the ceiling. It needs paint. Mom's been saying she was going to get the house painted for two years, but it never happens.

Sweet Caroline comes in and sits on the edge of the bed. The mattress creaks a little. Not much. She doesn't weigh much.

Without a word, she lies down and presses her body into mine. I turn on my side and wrap my arm around her.

I smell the trace of lavender oil on the pillow mixing with the fruit shampoo scent of Sweet Caroline's hair.

It's the smell of my family.

After a while, I hear the sound of a key in the front door followed by Dad cursing.

"How the hell does this thing—"

He doesn't know the lock is old and doesn't work right. You have to turn the knob half a turn or the key won't engage.

Finally, he gets it, and the door swings open and slams against the wall too hard. Mom hates it when we slam the door. I told her she should install a doorstop instead of yelling all the time, but she said it was our responsibility to take care of our home, not some piece of rubber's.

Dad curses again and closes the door.

Sweet Caroline is snoring softly in the bed next to me.

I press her shoulder.

"Dad's here," I say.

"Okay," she says.

But she doesn't move.

"We should go," I say.

"To Dad's."

"We can make it work."

"We make it work two days a month, Sanskrit. I'm not naïve. I know it's not a thirty days per month kind of experience."

She's right. But I don't say it. I say, "Let's go and find out."

She rolls away from me.

"I've got everything on a list.
I just need to find the list."

That's what Dad says. He stands there patting his pockets while Sweet Caroline and I wait for him.

We're in the living room surrounded by boxes.

"Everything we need to do is on the list," Dad says. "The packing, the organizing, the whatchamacallits. I just need to remember where I put it."

"Did you look in your back pockets?" Sweet Caroline says.

"I did," Dad says.

"Did you check your sock?" I say. Another of Dad's favorite hiding places.

"Let me think for a minute," Dad says.

Sweet Caroline clenches my arm, her fingers digging in. I can feel her starting to panic.

"It will be okay," I tell her.

Dad looks around the room, confused.

The doorbell rings, and the three of us jump.

Sweet Caroline looks at me hopefully.

Is it Mom? Did she change her mind?

I rush to the door. It's Herschel.

"On my way to Shabbos services," he says. "I know it's a big day. I hope you don't mind that I—"

"I'm glad you're here," I say.

"Good Shabbos," he says, and gives me a big hug.

He pokes his head in the front door.

"Good Shabbos, Zuckerman family," he says.

Dad gives him a wave. Sweet Caroline forces a smile.

"Shall we sit outside for a minute?" he says.

"I'll be right back," I tell Dad.

I squat down on the front stoop. Herschel pulls a handkerchief from his suit pocket and brushes off the stairs so he won't get his black pants dirty.

"Your mom?" Herschel says.

"She left a few minutes ago."

"How are you doing?"

"I don't know yet."

He takes off his hat, fans his forehead with it.

"I was thinking a lot about you last night. Your situation," he says.

"You mean school?"

"Not so much that. There are other schools. Other places to learn. You can always live a Jewish life. Nothing can prevent that if it's what you want."

"True," I say. "If it's what I want."

"I was thinking more about your mother leaving."

"What about her?"

"Did you ask her to stay?"

"It's not that simple."

"Why not?" Herschel says.

I think about that. I've tried all these way to manipulate Mom, change her mind, get her to see that we're worth it. But did I ever ask her to stay?

What do you want? Mom said in the car yesterday.

But I didn't answer. You shouldn't have to ask your own mother to be a mother, should you?

"What does it matter now?" I say. "She left us. It's too late."

"It's never too late," Herschel says.

"What about God's will?" I say. "If it's God's will for her to go, there's nothing I can do to keep her here. You've said as much yourself."

"Since when do you believe in God?" he says.

And then he smiles.

I glance through the open door behind me. Sweet Caroline is crying on the sofa while Dad rubs her back in little circles. He looks like he's about to cry himself.

Maybe Herschel's right. Maybe it isn't too late.

I jump up.

"Dad! Start the car," I shout.

"We have to pack your stuff first," he says. "The list says—"

"Forget the list. We have to go now."

Sweet Caroline looks at me like I'm crazy.

"Where are we going?" Dad says.

"We're going to get Mom back," I say.

Sweet Caroline leaps off the sofa.

"Let's go!" she shouts.

We race to the car. Herschel follows us.

"What are you doing?" I say to him. "It's Shabbat. You can't be in a car."

"I can if it's life or death," he says.

"Red lights are optional."

That's what Dad says as we shoot through the intersection accompanied by a chorus of honking horns.

"Careful, Daddy," Sweet Caroline says.

Dad snorts and drives faster. He slides through stop signs, speeds up when he sees yellow lights, tailgates, and passes on the right. He gets us to the airport in record time. I've never been so grateful to have a maniac driver for a father.

He pulls up to the white loading area in front of the Tom Bradley International Terminal, and I'm out of the car before it even stops, Herschel and Sweet Caroline racing along behind me.

"I'll catch up to you!" Dad shouts after us.

We're heading for the security check-in when I realize we're in trouble.

"Boarding passes, please," the TSA agent says. He's tall and serious, a fifty-year-old guy who looks like a presidential candidate, a great mane of white hair on top of his head.

"We don't have boarding passes," I say. "We're trying to get to our mother before she leaves the country."

The agent looks us over. I'm sweating through my T-shirt, Sweet Caroline is fidgeting next to me and marching in place, and Herschel is in full Jewish garb, nervously spinning his hat on his head. We're like an airport security training poster.

"I'm sorry," he says. "I can't let you through."

"We lost our mom," Sweet Caroline says. She starts to cry. It's gotten us through a lot of jams in the past.

Not this time.

"Rules and regulations," the TSA agent says, holding up his hand in a *stop* gesture. "I'll call it in. We'll make an announcement so your mother will know where to find you."

"You don't understand," Sweet Caroline says.

"We have to get through!" I say, a little too loudly, because the TSA agent stands up from his chair and fingers the radio on his shoulder.

"I need you to take a step back," he says firmly.

His partner stops what he's doing and stands up, too, bracing for trouble.

"We're going to get arrested," Sweet Caroline says, panic in her voice.

"Why would you be arrested?" the agent says. He reaches towards something on his belt. Restraining cuffs.

Saying you're going to get arrested in an airport these days pretty much guarantees that it's going to happen.

I look at Herschel. His eyes are closed and he's praying.

"Not now," I say, and I nudge him.

He holds up a finger for me to wait, his eyes still closed.

He finishes, then opens his eyes. He seems calmer. He says to the TSA agent, "Please, sir, may I have a word with you?"

The TSA agent looks him up and down.

Herschel motions for us to step back, and we do.

The TSA agent nods once. He and Herschel step to the side to converse.

Sweet Caroline clasps my elbow, her fingers digging into my flesh.

"We have to hurry," she says.

"I know, I know," I say.

I keep imagining Mom getting on the plane, the plane taxiing out slowly, then taking off just as we get there. If we ever get there. It's not looking good.

The TSA agent argues with Herschel, but Herschel remains calm. I can't hear what he's saying, but he keeps talking, smoothing his *payis* with long strokes.

Just when I think it's a lost cause, the TSA agent steps back and Herschel motions for us to come towards them.

"I'm Episcopalian," the agent is saying to Herschel as we get to them.

"God bless you, Edward," Herschel says to him, and they shake hands.

"Follow me, kids," the agent says. "Open it, Jerry!"

The gate clicks, and we're suddenly bypassing the security check in.

"Me plus three," the agent shouts as we race past a phalanx of police officers.

Before I can even understand what's happened, we're running through the airport with the TSA agent shouting, "Clear a path!" to the people in front of us.

People jump out of the way and let us pass.

"Left turn," the agent shouts, and we race down the corridor.

We burst into the hall that feeds into the boarding gates.

"64B," I shout, and we head for the gate, the agent leading the way.

When we get there, it's already empty. The gate agent is closing the door.

"We're too late," I say.

"What your mother's name?" the TSA agent says.

"Rebekah Zuckerman," I say.

He runs to the gate agent, says a few words to her, and she unlocks the door. He disappears down the gangway. We're left there looking at one another.

"Is this the right flight?" Herschel says.

"Maybe we missed it," Sweet Caroline says.

"I don't think so," I say.

A minute passes, but it feels like hours.

Mom peeks her head out of the door. She looks around, confused, until she sees us.

"Oh my God," she says, and she runs over and throws her arms around me and Sweet Caroline.

"I thought I wouldn't get to say good-bye to you," Mom says.

"Me, too. I'm sorry, Mom."

She hugs me even harder. Then she notices Herschel behind us.

"You brought Herschel?" she says. "How did you all get here?"

"It's a long story," I say.

I put my hand on Sweet Caroline's back.

"Give us a minute?" I say softly.

She nods and steps back to where Herschel is waiting.

Mom says, "I thought a lot about what you said, Sanskrit. About the choice I'm making. I thought I knew what I was doing, but I feel confused now."

"Confused about what?"

"About India. About leaving my family."

"Really?"

She looks back towards the gate, then at me.

"There you are," Dad says, jogging up behind us escorted by the other TSA agent. "Jesus H., you can't pee in this place without a secret service detail."

"Your father is here, too?" Mom says.

"He brought us."

Mom looks surprised. She takes a curl of my hair between her fingers. Her skin is cool against my neck.

"I'm lost," Mom says.

Her voice is small and high like a little girl's.

"Tell me what to do," she says.

This is what Herschel was talking about, the moment I can ask Mom to stay. I'm trying to form the words when the guru appears at the gate door with the agent behind him.

I expect the guru to come out and grab Mom, but he doesn't. He stays there, framed in the doorway. He smiles at me—a kind smile like he's glad to see me here. But how can he be glad?

I look behind me at Sweet Caroline, Herschel, and Dad.

"Sanskrit?" Mom says. She holds my face in her hands. "Aren't you going to say anything?"

All I have to do is tell Mom I want her to stay. That I need her here. *We* need her.

She'll stay. I can feel it.

But then what?

Will she suddenly love Sweet Caroline and me like she's supposed to? Will she be a mother to us?

Will she be happy?

The guru is watching us, giving us space.

I hate him so much.

But I try to see him through Mom's eyes. He is her future. Her spiritual partner. Her chance for love.

I can barely think of him like that, but barely is enough. Because it gives me some perspective on Mom. She's been happy since she met him. I haven't seen her like this in years.

No. I've never seen her like this.

I open my mouth to tell Mom to stay, and something comes over me. A different feeling. Like the feeling I had at Dr. Prem's.

I feel lighter. I can breathe.

I notice the carpet, that awful pattern you see in hotel lobbies, airports, and other public spaces. I follow the lines of the pattern. All roads lead to Mom. All roads lead away. It depends on your perspective.

Mom is lost. She said it herself. Nobody leaves her kids unless she's lost.

I pull Mom closer to me, so close that my face is right up against her ear.

"I want you to go to India," I say. "I want you to find yourself."

"Do you mean it?"

I nod.

Mom bursts into tears.

"I want you to find out who you are so you can come back and be our mother."

"That's the nicest thing you've ever said to me."

Mom cries so hard that she grabs onto me for

balance. She makes blubbering sounds, and snot comes out of her nose. It's not pretty.

She sinks down to her knees in front of me, still holding on.

"Why are you crying?" I say.

"I'm so happy," Mom says. "And sad, too. I'm everything all at once."

Mom pulls me down to her and covers my face with kisses.

"Love and Sanskrit," Mom says. "That's how I'll remember this day. The two gifts you've given me."

The guru comes forward. "We have to go," he says.

He puts his hands on Mom's shoulders and she rises. I stay there, sitting on the ground.

"I love you, Sanskrit," Mom says.

"I love you, too, Mom."

She kisses me, then goes to Sweet Caroline.

"Don't go, Mommy! Please!" Sweet Caroline says.

Mom hugs her.

"Sanskrit, do something!" Sweet Caroline screams, not understanding what's happening.

Mom envelops her in a hug.

The guru and I look at each other.

He presses his palms together at chest level.

"*Namaste*," he says, and he bows deeply to me.

"*Namaste*," I say.

"Closing the door," the gate agent says.

Mom and the guru join hands and walk onto the

gangway. The agent closes and locks the door behind them. The TSA agent stands by the door, sniffling and rubbing at his eyes.

The hall fills with people. People leave, more people come. It's the rhythm of the airport. I sit down on the floor as people pass around me.

I feel pressure on my back. It's Sweet Caroline. She hits me.

"I thought you were going to make her to stay!" she says.

She slams me on the back.

"I hate you!" she says.

The punches become slaps, and then Sweet Caroline collapses into tears.

"She needed to go," I whisper. "She'll be back. I know she will."

"How do you know?"

"I just do."

She slumps down to the floor behind me and puts her legs on the outside of mine. She hugs me tightly, her arms around my chest. I hear her sniffling and feel her nose running wet through my shirt.

Dad is watching us, unsure what to do. I can see that he wants to help, he just doesn't know how. He finally takes a step towards us, but I give him the *one minute* finger.

I shift around so I'm facing Sweet Caroline. We hug each other, curled together on the floor.

"Your makeup is running," I say.

Sweet Caroline dabs at her eyes.

"Does it look bad?"

"It just looks like you've been crying. You shouldn't be wearing makeup, anyway. You're only twelve."

"Give me a break," she says. "All the girls wear it."

I say, "If all the girls jumped off a bridge, would you?"

"That's a lame Dad line," Sweet Caroline says.

We stand up. Dad waits for us across the way with a big goofy smile on his face.

"I've already got a father," Sweet Caroline says. "Sort of."

"Good point," I say.

"But I could use a brother," she says.

"You've got one."

She holds my hand.

"We have to take care of each other," I say. "It's not going to be easy."

Herschel is talking to Dad now. It looks like one of those man-to-man talks Herschel specializes in.

An engine roars as Mom's plane pulls back from the gate. Sweet Caroline turns and runs to the window. I join her. We stand together, watching until Mom disappears.

"We're truly sorry
it didn't work out."

This is what the dean says in his office the next day. I would accuse him of grandstanding, of trying to look good in front of everyone, but there's nobody here except him and me.

It's my exit interview from Jewish school.

"We had high hopes for you," he says. "Not just because we wanted you to do well, but because we know how much it meant to your zadie."

That last part really stings.

"I was a long shot," I say. "Even I knew that."

"There are no long shots in God's world," the dean says. "If God's reach is infinite, then what does it matter how far we are from him? The greatest distance is nothing to the Almighty."

"That's a nice thought," I say.

"You don't believe it."

"I don't."

"That's where faith comes in, Aaron."

"Sanskrit. My name is Sanskrit, but you always call me Aaron."

"Your Hebrew name is also your name. *Ah-roan*."

He uses the Hebrew pronunciation.

"No, it's not. My grandfather pushed a Hebrew name on me, but it's not my name. My mother gave me my name, and it's the name I want to be called."

"I stand corrected," he says.

The dean stands up, extends his hand.

"I wish you luck, Sanskrit."

For a moment, I think about walking away without shaking his hand. My grand exit from Jewish school. But the dean is being a mensch, so I will, too.

I shake the man's hand.

"Thanks for trying," I say.

"That's my job," he says. "It was not so difficult with you, Sanskrit. Not as difficult as you would believe."

"I don't know about that."

I think about Mom, how difficult it was for her to be my mother. I always assumed it was because I was difficult to begin with. But what if the dean is right?

It's not that I'm difficult, it's just that Mom has trouble being a mom.

"Good-bye, dean," I say.

I head for the door.

"Even though you're leaving us, don't leave God," the dean says.

When I get outside, Dorit is sitting at her desk in the main office. She follows me with her eyes.

"What?" I say.

"I rubbed your back," she says angrily. "What do you have to say for yourself?"

"Guilty as charged."

Her face softens.

"Honesty," she says. "That's a good beginning for you."

There's nothing else to say.

That's what I think as I walk through school for the last time.

Nothing to say to Herschel. Nothing to The Initials.

It's all been said.

I walk past my cabinet for the last time.

I go out to the parking lot. I look across to the synagogue.

On one side is the school, on the other the synagogue. Cars in between. The secular and the spiritual, separated by the real world of gas prices.

I walk out to the street, and I stop.

I look back at the synagogue. For some reason, I want to see it again. One last time before I go.

Jewish jail.

That's what it felt like when I was a kid. My parents would drag me to services on Saturday mornings. Not Mom. Not anymore. But in the past when she and Dad were still pretending to be Jewish for *der kinder*.

They'd drag me to synagogue for services on Shabbat morning. They'd drop me off in a classroom with the other kids before going into the big synagogue.

We'd have a separate and supposedly fun children's service, designed to make us fall in love with Judaism.

The Hebrew school's idea of fun? We sat on a cold linoleum floor, squirming and hating it, while they taught us Bible stories and made us clap and sing *Dayenu* and other Jewish songs.

When I was finally old enough to be in the synagogue, what did I discover?

A group of adults sitting on barely padded benches, squirming and hating it.

Jewish jail. It's a life sentence.

That was the real lesson of synagogue. It never ends.

Not true. It ends now. It ends for me.

No more Jewish school. No more services. No more hard floors or benches.

It took me getting thrown out of school, but I'm free now.

Like Herschel said, I could go somewhere else. There are plenty of private Jewish schools that will take me if I can afford the tuition. It wouldn't have to be in L.A. I could go over to Pasadena or down to South Bay. Up to Northridge. There are other schools, more liberal schools, plenty of places to spend Zadie Zuckerman's money.

But Dad and I talked about it last night, and he

came around to my way of thinking. I'm going to be a public school kid again. I promised him I'd go to a state school and apply for financial aid when it came time for college. That probably means UCLA instead of Brandeis, but it's a small price to pay for freedom. The dean thinks God has an infinite reach? He never met Zadie Zuckerman. Zadie was reaching all the way from the grave to make me a Jew in his own image, but he failed.

It's a great day for me. An even greater day for the Tay-Sachs research community.

I walk through the main hall of the synagogue. Portraits of the executive committee look down on me. Then portraits of the building committee. Then portraits of high-level donors. Lots of glaring Jews with white hair.

I imagine Zadie's portrait among them. What would he say if he could see me now?

On the opposite wall is a Chagall print of a somber Jewish man contemplating the Torah while his goat looks on. An angel dances high above them. A fiddle sits unplayed on the ground.

Man trapped between heaven and earth. In one place, thinking of the other.

Maybe that's how it was in little Russian villages in the nineteenth century, but that's not how it is now. At least not for me.

I arrive at the dark carved-wood doors of the

synagogue. I've walked through these doors several hundred times in the last two years. I've hated every time.

But it feels different now with nobody around. No ushers reminding me to put a *kippah* on my head. No jostling for the good seats.

I touch the door, let my fingers trace the carved wood.

I go inside.

There's nobody here.

The pews are ready for services, the prayer books stuck in little pockets. At the front of the synagogue is the raised carpeted bima, the stage where the rabbi and cantor stand. It's just high enough that everyone in the synagogue can see them. In the Jewish religion, we're taught that there is no intermediary needed to reach God. The rabbi does not stand above you. He stands among you. You connect to God together.

But everyone wants to see the show, so they have the bima.

Above it is the Eternal Light. The flame of the Jewish people. The reminder of God. It never goes out because it's connected to a gas line with its own power source.

HaShem is a pilot light. It's like praying to your stove.

I sit down in a pew. It's nice in the syngagogue when it's quiet, when nobody's around to blow their noses, say stupid things, daven too much, slip mints to their family during the sermon, forget to turn off their cell phones.

I think about the life of the synagogue and the culture that surrounds it. It usually seems absurd to me, a lot of noise that adds up to nothing. But now I think of it a little differently.

Everyone is trying. Herschel is trying. My teachers. The rabbi, the dean, my whole school. They're all trying.

Outside of school, too.

Mom is trying. Dr. Prem is trying.

Judi Jacobs and Barry Goldwasser. The yoga mommies.

Even the guru.

They're all trying to feel connected to something bigger than them.

I lean forward in the pew. It's hard wood. Not comfortable at all.

But I like it in here. It's quiet. Kind of nice. I never knew that before.

I never knew people were trying, and I never knew it was nice in the synagogue.

"Great Spirit—" I say.

And then I stop. Because I don't know what a great spirit is. That's Mom's word.

"Infinite and Divine," I say, because that's how Dr. Prem says it. But it doesn't feel right to me.

"God," I say.

I don't know what God is either, but I don't hate the word.

I say it again. Out loud in the empty synagogue.

"God."

The space feels less empty.

"Thank you," I say. "Not because things worked out, because they didn't. I pretty much got screwed on the Mom and Judi Jacobs front. And I won't be graduating from B-Jew. So I really can't thank you for that."

My leg is falling asleep. I move on the pew, shift from one butt cheek to the other.

"And I can't thank you for this pew, which is hard and hurts my *tuchas*."

The eternal flame flickers. I wonder if God is pissed at me for saying *tuchas* in synagogue. Maybe he hates that I used a slang term for *ass*, or maybe he loves that I spoke Yiddish at all. But I can't believe in a God like that, one who hates or loves according to an obscure set of rules. I have to believe in one I can say anything to. I can tell him the truth, I can be myself, and he doesn't blink.

"I can't thank you for making things work out, but maybe I can thank you for being with me while they didn't."

Was God with me?

I close my eyes and think about it for a while. I don't get any answers.

Instead of pushing through and trying to figure it

out, I hold the question in my head like the guru taught me. I sit with it. I sit with the idea of God.

After a while I look at my phone. A half hour has passed. I think it's the longest I've ever been in a synagogue voluntarily.

I should leave now, but I don't want to.

I want to stay.

I want to sit with God a little longer.